*Time & Time*

# *Time &*
# *Time Again*

*Jacky Gray*

*To Keith and all the other wonderful time-travellers in the Broadhall Social Club.*

*Find out more at:*
*https://jroauthor.co.uk/*
*https://hengistpeoplehorse.blogspot.co.uk/*
*https://www.facebook.com/HengistPeopleOfTheHorse*

*Subscribe to Jacky's newsletter to find out the latest news and deals and receive your FREE Bonus Extras:*
*https://eepurl.com/b5ZScH*

# Contents

# Prologue – The Monster

Savage Caverns

    Alex the Brave (Ben) – a Celtic warrior

    Jinx the Bard (Kev) – a Gnome halfling

    Storyteller (Isaac) – a Dungeon Master

    Niamh of the Forest (Georgie) – a Druid

    Anwyn the Ranger (Jen) – an Elf

"Wait. Something doesn't smell right." Alex the Brave held his cloak over his nose and the others halted, gathering around the meagre light from the torch he carried. "The fetid stench suggests a foul entity resides nearby."

"Whizz is fretting – we must be close." The tricksy Jinx took the sack from his back, cradling it close as he crooned a soothing ditty to the distressed creature inside.

"Take care, questors." The storyteller paused, needing the full attention of his four charges, waiting until the bard glanced up and gestured for him to continue.

Filling his expression with the required amount of gravitas, the storyteller, known to some as the Dungeon Master, lowered his voice. "You must all proceed with every fibre of your being on alert." He directed a question at the two females of the party. "What can you sense?"

Niamh of the Forest pointed down to where the others could barely make out the broken stones lying on the rough ground. "Darkvision shows me the trail of destruction the heinous creature has left in its wake as it slithered to its lair. The track stops a few paces before the end of the cave."

Anwyn tucked long, white hair behind her pointed ears and concentrated. "My ranger hearing has picked up the

1

shallow, even breathing of a sleeping animal." She glanced at the others. "Should I remind you of the dangers?"

"Please." Jinx gave an appealing smile. "You gave so much detail I've forgotten which one is for which beast."

Ignoring his charm, she pressed on. "All the clues, in particular the weasel's reaction, confirm it *is* the basilisk, whose most potent weapon is its killing glare."

Alex pulled a mirror from his weapon sack. "But if I deflect it with this, he will be destroyed, right?"

"Not instantly, and not if it misses his gaze. Never get complacent with these creatures, because they have a full armoury, including breath so noxious it can burn, as we saw from the scorched grass outside the cave."

"I remember now. You said one man died because as he stabbed one, its poison sped up the spear and killed not only the man but his horse too." Jinx shuddered. "So apart from the mirror, how do we kill it?"

"This is where Whizz the weasel comes in. The smell of his urine is known to kill this breed."

Jinx hugged the sack as the creature's head popped out. "Surely there's another way? I've became quite attached to the wee fellow. Will he not be in terrible danger?"

Seeing Anwyn falter, the storyteller suggested she could do an intelligence check, reminding how a ranger's proficiency bonus doubled when they recalled information about monsters. She rolled the twenty-sided dice, which landed on a nine, but she also had an advantage, which meant she could roll again and choose the better score. Everyone cheered when she threw a thirteen on the d20 dice.

The Dungeon Master added in the bonuses. "A total of

eighteen – more than enough. As you know, the basilisk is weakened by the herb rue and can be killed by the sound of a rooster's crow."

"You don't happen to have a rooster about your person, Niamh?" Jinx winked.

She rolled her eyes. "No, but I do have rue, which by the way, will help your furry friend recover." She dug into her backpack, pulling out a linen parcel which she unrolled.

Anwyn sniffed the herb, recoiling. "If it helps recovery, would it not afford extra protection if he ate some first?"

"Genius!" In his excitement, Jinx forgot to speak the common tongue.

Moments when the players became immersed in the quest made it all worthwhile for any Dungeon Master. With a gratified smile, he described the action.

*"As the weasel feasted on the rue and drank his fill, Alex arranged his mirror for optimum cover of the entrance hole. Niamh prepared a bough of the herb and lowered it carefully in."*

As he spoke, she mimed the actions – truly a gratifying addition to the team. He continued.

*"After several moments, she retrieved it and all the green leaves had turned white, showing the creature lived. The gnome, Jinx, gave Whizz a final hug ..."*

He glared until his least favourite questor stirred himself to do the necessary.

*"... and the weasel squeezed past the mirror, scurrying around squirting its stinking piss all over the surfaces and even on the creature itself. The beast squealed so terribly the four friends had to cover their ears."*

He paused as they complied.

*"Finally, when the deadly sound died, Niamh lowered another branch of rue which came back as green as it went in, indicating the death of the monster. Whizz jumped out of the lair to be met with much appreciation and a tasty treat Jinx had saved for him."*

Donning suitable gauntlets, Alex retrieved the monster's body, stowing it in an impenetrable pouch. "We should return to the earl."

The storyteller tutted. "While you were in the lower cavern, the basilisk's death scream caused a landfall in the tunnel you used on the way here."

"Is it passable?" Alex shaded his eyes, peering into the gloom.

"No. Your only option is the left fork, which leads to a massive chasm with no bridge across and only a four-inch ledge which has crumbled away in several places."

# Ch 1 – Elf-height-gate

2017 – Season 1

Ben's whole mouth felt tender after fifteen minutes' attention from the hygienist, but in his absence, world war three had broken out.

Isaac had his back to the door, and the rest of the development team surrounded him like marauding renegades, their animosity evident. Several voices shouted at once and Isaac had retreated behind his arms, raised as though holding an imaginary shield.

"What the hell's going on?" Ben's question had them pausing like a freeze frame.

"Blame this maniac." Oso, the Swedish guy whose family owned the house Ben shared with a couple of other lads, fell naturally into the role of mouthpiece, being the next most senior. "After weeks telling us not to bother, he's saying every line change needs a peer review."

Ben didn't want to admit he'd not heard about this modification to the procedure, which was extremely worrying as he was quality assurance liaison for the team. *No doubt why Isaac hadn't mentioned it to him.* As far as Ben was concerned, nothing had changed.

But pointing this out would only fan the flames. "Okay, guys. This sounds like a miscommunication. Can I suggest we return to reviewing *every* change from now on? If you're altering a module, review any recent modifications which don't have a review number logged."

"But it'll be a right pain and we don't need it in the release crunch." Oso shook his head.

"Yeah. *He's* the one who cocked up, so he should pay the penalty." Kev, Ben's mate from uni, sought backing from the others, who readily gave it. Trying to keep his personal preferences out of it, Ben couldn't help but side with his housemate who'd crossed swords with Isaac several times since joining the team. But Kev had suffered once too often and wanted retribution.

Feeling everyone's eyes on him, their body language suggesting a shared grievance, Ben had to come up with something to satisfy them all, while maintaining the semblance of supporting the chain of command. "If you think back, there's been little brand new code written in the past few months while we've had a purge on the backlog of bugs thrown up by the beta trials." His gaze rested on every person in turn.

"The test team always soak test every bug fix, so it's unlikely any further errors would have slipped through." Isaac smirked.

Ben eyed him coolly. "But this is not an acceptable justification for not reviewing."

Frowning, he wondered what other shortcuts had gone on to expedite the release. The QA role meant his neck would be on the block if the external inspectors detected a glitch in any of the processes. Something niggled at the back of his mind, but he couldn't connect the dots.

"Right lads, back to work." The formidable command made them all jump. "Isaac, Ben. My office. Pronto."

*Wtf?* He hadn't heard Rollason, the big boss, enter the office, and wondered how much he'd observed. Following them into the guy's office, they sat in the purposely uncomfortable plastic chairs while the guy settled into his captain's chair. According to some bullshit corporate research about manager's efficiency, the hard chairs were intended to encourage visitors not to outstay their welcome. "So, Isaac. I take it the directive wasn't well received?"

"No more than a Christian thrown to a pack of half-starved lions. They wanted blood – specifically mine. But I only did what–"

"Thank you. How do you think they took it, Ben?"

"I wasn't there. Dental appointment."

Grunting, he scowled at Isaac. "Summarise this morning's meeting in two hundred words or less. In my inbox by one o'clock, please." He waved him away.

As his team leader exited, Ben got the impression he was used to being dealt with so brusquely. But the manager's focus had moved on.

"Dental appointment, eh? A filling?"

"No, the hygienist." His hand involuntarily snuck up to his lower jaw where she'd touched a nerve.

"Don't worry, you're not in trouble. This company applauds staff who prioritise their healthcare. It's obvious you work at keeping yourself fit and active. Healthy body, healthy mind and the like. Tell me what happened when you reached the office."

Ben glossed over the worst aspects of what he'd witnessed, taking the emotion out to give an objective account.

"So the section clerk overreacted when she rang my secretary to suggest Isaac might be in danger?"

Ben's eyebrows beetled. "I know these lads, sir. They

7

put up with a lot, but I'm confident not one of them would resort to physical violence no matter what the provocation."

"Aha! And there we have it." The triumphant gleam made Ben realise how badly he'd been played.

Rocks and hard places sprang to mind as he re-examined his words, trying to think of something he could have said which wouldn't have landed Isaac or his team in the brown stuff.

Rollason regarded him over steepled fingers. "Trust me; you couldn't have done any more than you did. I've suspected for a while Isaac is a round peg in a square hole, and today confirmed how little respect he commands from his team."

"Sir?"

"Don't try to defend him. You, on the other hand, are a leader they would follow into the breach."

Ignoring the hyperbole, Ben's instinct was to deny, but his manager held up a palm to silence him.

"I watched the way they responded to your suggestions, and the clever way you diffused the emotions which were running hotter than a formula 1 engine. How would you feel about a promotion to team leader?"

"What about Isaac?" Despite his quirks, the guy didn't deserve summary demotion.

"Your loyalty does you credit, but I believe he'll welcome a transfer to the spec team with open arms."

"He'll do well with the other planet-sized brains. His particular talents are much better suited to their ivory tower existence."

"Very apt, but please don't propagate that description –

we have enough problems between the departments as it is. Although with you heading up development I'm sure the interface will improve drastically."

"What about my QA duties? I won't have time to give them the attention they deserve."

"True. I suspect you've been doing far more than deputy TL for a while. Do you have a suitable replacement in mind?"

"Oso is the most experienced and the guys respect him."

"He would be my choice. But I think we'll separate out the QA function. If I offered it to Kev, would he accept?"

Ben did a double-take. "He's more than capable, but so are the others and they've been there longer."

"The post has no remuneration and is a gigantic pain in the arse as you can no doubt testify. Should suit him down to the ground."

Ben deadpanned. "A little responsibility won't hurt."

"My thoughts exactly. I think we'll work well together."

As he left the office, Ben finally felt vindicated about bringing Kev into the company – for a while it had been touch-and-go. The decision hadn't been easy, particularly given his "unconscious death wish," as one of his girlfriends had put it. But like a best mate should, Ben had kept him sober enough to take his finals and, when he returned from his round-the-world travels, wangled him an interview at the firm. He'd even persuaded the sceptical Oso to give him a trial place in the coolest of house-shares.

So far, Kev hadn't let him down, but there was plenty of time – he could be a loose cannon at the best of times. From the moment Kev joined the team, Isaac had taken pot-shots at him. It started with remarks about his scruffy appearance and messy desk, and then got personal, as Isaac took great delight in berating him about his "pedestrian" code. Despite extreme provocation, Kev had controlled his temper, but it all came to a head during his first peer review over a year ago.

"Really, you're introducing variables for the character heights? How ridiculous is that? They're never going to alter the height of an elf, it's set in stone. It uses far fewer instructions if you hard-wire the number in."

"Yes, but with each one taking nanoseconds, it won't make a discernible difference." Ben managed to veto Isaac's suggestion, pointing out it would have amounted to substantial changes over all the affected modules.

Not used to having his opinion challenged, Isaac pouted and griped his way through the last three procedures, disappearing promptly at the end.

Kev blinked as the door slammed. "Does he always sulk when he doesn't get his own way?"

Ben rolled his eyes. "You have no idea. I knew he'd have a go, so I put my name down so I could support you. Didn't want you losing confidence on your first substantial piece of code."

"'preciate it, mate."

Unfortunately, it put a target on Kev's back and led to quips about Mickey Mouse code and public taunts that Isaac could replace any ten lines of Kev's code with three. It finally stopped when Isaac moved to the spec team.

One of Ben's first tasks was to recruit some new people,

and this went reasonably well until it came to Jennifer Paulson. Reading through her CV, he had an inkling she might be trouble. When Oso led the morning tour around the building, he'd singled her out as a front runner, and she had the last interview slot before lunch.

When they were seated, he got straight to business. "Thank you for coming, Miss Paulson. Before we start, do you have any questions about this morning's tour?"

"Yes. How come there's a men's loo on every floor, but women have to go up or down a floor to pee?"

He struggled not to squirm at her militant tone. "A legacy, I'm afraid. You may have spotted around twenty percent are females, but it used to be less than one percent."

"But the company hasn't moved with the times when it comes to providing for their comfort."

"Because of the extension. It should be finished by the end of the year and we'll have a big re-shuffle—"

"And I'm supposed to hold it till then?"

"Not at all." Trying to think on his feet, he leaned forward. "How would you fix it?"

She folded her arms. "Is that what they teach on interviewing courses these days? Fire the awkward questions back at the candidate?"

He couldn't help the truthful knee-jerk reaction. "I've no idea. I haven't been on the course yet."

"Really? You're a couple of years older than me and only just made manager?"

Shit. This wasn't going to plan at all.

Her face cracked. "Gotcha. Best reaction so far."

"What the what?"

A cheeky grin. "I'll fill in my own expletive. You really are green, aren't you?"

For a moment, Ben imagined Isaac's reaction – or even Kev's – to her assertive attitude. But growing up in a house full of strong women had taught him not to take himself too seriously. Throwing away the expected umbrage, he settled back in his chair, meeting her amused gaze. "Jennifer–"

"Jen, please."

He inclined his head. "I can tell you don't particularly care about working for this firm, so I suggest you take your very reasonable demands to a firm who have prioritised catering for an increasing female workforce. You may be the highest qualified applicant, but we value teamwork above intellectual ability and flexibility over arrogance."

"Are they not recording this for training purposes?"

"What do you think?" *God, he hoped not.*

"Then they should use it to show engineers how to grow a pair. You've single-handedly put Gaming UK at the top of my list of prospective workplaces."

"Good for you." A cool glance. "Always assuming we offer you the job."

"I think you'll find it's a given. Can we start over?"

"If you tell me your solution to the loos problem."

"Simple. Until they get their fingers out, the first floor will be unisex like they have in America."

It never happened, despite her uncle being on the board of directors but, from that moment on, things improved.

When a potentially deal-breaking report came in – late – from marketing, Ben called Kev and Jen into a meeting. He outlined the last-minute change before next month's massive launch in an Asian country. "Apparently, initial beta trials have discovered that in their culture, elves are not the tall, blond creatures of many modern incarnations."

"As popularised in Lord of the Rings."

"Among others. They see them as small, impish beings, more like dwarves and gnomes."

"They couldn't have told us this earlier?" Kev scowled.

"And you've never made a mistake? We'll need to add in a country-specific variable wherever elf-height appears."

"That's a one line change in my modules." Kev preened. "Unless we make it a case statement for other countries."

Ben nodded. "Good idea. The more future-proofing the better. It's the first time we've come across this, but as we gain footholds in new territories, those are the sort of question the specification guys should be asking. We'll need someone from the spec team–"

"Not Isaac, surely." Kev held up crossed fingers.

"'fraid so. This is his area of expertise."

Jen frowned. "Is this Isaac as bad as they say?"

"Depends what you've heard."

"Let's say difficult to work with and a tad arrogant."

Kev grinned. "I'm guessing your diplomacy has cleaned up the language. The last word's normally git or twat and there's at least one swear-word first."

"Yep, you got it. Sounds like he doesn't play well with others."

As Kev laughed out loud, Isaac walked in and, spotting Jen, asked her to get him an Earl Grey tea.

Ben glared at him. "Jen's our latest recruit – she's taken over the maintenance of a lot of your modules. She'll need guidance to unravel your user-unfriendly code."

He rolled his eyes. "As I've often explained, there's always a trade-off between readability and efficiency."

"Yes, we know the arguments, but the difference is not evident to the average user."

Folding his arms, Isaac huffed. "This sounds trivial. Let's get on with it. You have the code there?"

Jen opened up her laptop. "I ran a search on the value you hard-wired into your modules. Fifty-three occurrences – a total nightmare to find and alter individually.

Isaac tutted. "Ever heard of global search and replace?"

She shot a scathing glance. "Under normal circumstances, it would work, but the way you have it set up, I can't do a replace-all because not every occurrence of the number refers to elf-height."

"What? How do you know?"

"Because she's so thorough, she checked the spec documents." Kev jumped in.

"And Kev's modules confirmed it. The list of character heights at the start show the same value has been used for several humanoid races, including humans."

"Oops." Isaac shrugged. "That's a bummer."

"It's way more than a bummer. If we don't get it right by Thursday, it could cost us the contract." Ben scowled.

"I'm sure if you get a few more guys on it, you'll sort it out." Isaac rose, gathering his things.

"You're going nowhere, mate." Kev stood, towering over him, almost nose-to-nose, and Isaac cringed back.

Ben didn't condone physical intimidation, but Kev had convinced him it sometimes got the job done more effectively than logical reasoning or appealing to a non-existent better nature. And this was definitely one of those.

As Isaac sat, Jen plied him with questions about each procedure, making copious notes which would end up as in-line comments improving the readability. Her serene, no-nonsense approach appealed to Isaac's rarely-seen generosity, mostly driven by a chance to show off his planet-sized coding skills.

At the end of the meeting, Isaac asked Ben for a word. "In private." He glared at the others, waiting till they left.

Ben expected a complaint about Kev's behaviour, so was blindsided by his question.

"I believe you're an experienced D&D player, who's your character?"

"Alex the Brave."

"A warrior, good. Barbarian, Orc or Elf?"

"Celtic." He glanced at his watch.

"Even better. What level?"

"Sorry, but I'm late for a meeting. Can we pick this up another time?" Sidestepping, he dashed off.

Isaac cornered him later, and Ben's response to the invitation lacked any enthusiasm. "I'm not sure. Kev and I played all the time at uni and we talked recently about finding a party to join."

"Sorry, but there's only one slot available."

"That's a hard no, then. It's both or neither."

"Really?" His expression suggested he hadn't realised the depth of their friendship. "What's his character?"

"He usually plays an elven sorcerer."

"We have many magicals. Does he have another one?"

"Jinx the Bard. He's a gnome halfling."

"A trickster, eh? Any combat skills?"

"Absolutely. Great with a short sword and crossbow."

"Unusual. It might work. We're due to start a new campaign next week – you could come along and meet the others and take it from there."

Their presence turned out to be fortuitous, as two of the other players had decided to resign, but agreed to stay on to see how it went with the new additions.

Halfway through the campaign, it became obvious they were no longer fully committed as one or both turned up late or missed sessions completely. Isaac manipulated the quest so it ended several weeks early and, when the pair resigned, he asked Ben if he thought Jen might join.

Ben had only recently found out she played and shrugged. "You can but ask." Grinning at the potential for fun, he made sure he was working nearby when Isaac approached her desk that afternoon.

"I hear you're a level nine ranger. Quite impressive."

She took her time finishing her immediate task, hitting ctrl-s before glaring at him.

"I can see you're busy so I'll be brief. I need a fourth player for my party and a ranger would fit nicely."

"I hope you find one, then." Her gaze returned to the screen.

He cleared his throat. "You do realise that was an invitation? I'm sure Benjamin and Kevin would be thrilled if you joined." When she didn't glance up, he continued.

"Although maybe you'd think twice because you do have to work with them all day." He snickered.

With a sigh, she glanced at him. "Really? Ben and Kev are in a D&D party with you?"

He nodded. "It's my party."

"And no doubt you'll cry if you want to." With a twinkle in her eye, she returned to her work, clicking the mouse.

He scowled. "I don't get it. Why would I cry?"

"It's a song lyric. As you can see, I'm busy, but if you leave me a note with the time and place I'll consider it."

Jen was an excellent addition to the team bringing wisdom, intuition and one hundred percent commitment to the table. Obviously besotted, the third guy became utterly reckless in his efforts to outdo the others and impress her, asking her out after the second session. After a gentle rebuff, she exited, and Kev took him to one side, explaining Jen preferred girls. He took it badly, calling her some unsavoury names before stalking off, never to be seen again. Which left them back at four.

When Jen mentioned her housemate, Georgie, the lads were keen, but for some reason Isaac wasn't, and Ben put it down to the idea of having a second girl. However, when she turned out to be his long-lost cousin, he couldn't very well refuse. But her druid balanced the team perfectly, and the party worked well, allowing Isaac to develop increasingly complex and satisfying campaigns.

~*~

Georgie had grave misgivings about the whole thing when she found out it was Isaac's party. But she gave it a

17

go, surprised to find things which irritated her when they were young, no longer did. She couldn't decide whether she'd grown more tolerant with age or he'd changed. On balance, it was probably the latter – no doubt down to his relationship with his nan. She totally got this.

Her own mum had died when she was quite young and, because her dad spent months away on construction projects in the Middle East, she lived with her gran most of the time. Gran was deeply in touch with her gypsy roots, harking back to the values of Druid ancestors. Everything she did or bought showed reverence to Mother Earth, and she never wasted anything. Her council house had a zero carbon-footprint long before the term was ever invented.

Then social services in their wisdom, declared Gran in need of daily care, insisting she move into a care home so they could use her house for a large family of refugees. So the pair went to live with Georgie's dad, but after three days putting up with her wicked stepmother's continual bitching, Georgie spent her evenings scouring Craigslist, Gumtree and Sparerooms, where she found Jen.

Within minutes of meeting her, Georgie reckoned she must have done something splendid in another lifetime for the universe to see fit to hook her up with her twin. They quickly forged a deep bond, sharing experiences like an old married couple: shopping, cooking and eating together, and exploring the myriad of local dining establishments.

Georgie never tried putting a label on their relationship, but knew the love they shared was deeper than friendship and stronger than siblings. They were soul sisters.

Despite being a man-magnet, Jen kept them all at arm's

length while managing to treat them with genuine interest. Finally, she admitted to recently ending a long relationship with a nurse called Val, saying she wouldn't be ready to get back on the dating horse for a while. But the universe had other ideas, and when she got back together with Val, Georgie had no clue for several weeks. Their meetings were limited to long lunches because of Val's late shifts, so Georgie wasn't prepared when she opened the door to a tall, dark-haired nurse with liquid brown eyes.

"Is Jen around?" The cheeky grin put Georgie at a disadvantage, suggesting the sultry stranger knew all about her, and the next statement confirmed it. "You must be Georgie. I'm Val."

"I – I. But you're ..."

"Early, I'm afraid. We were supposed to meet in town, but my shift finished sooner than planned so I thought she might be up for a slight change of plans. Can I come in?"

"Sure." Georgie stepped back, treading on Jen's toes.

"Val. I wasn't expecting you. I should do a proper introduction."

"No need. Although I suspect I know a lot more about Georgie than you seem to have told her about me."

Staring at the six-foot, muscular frame, Georgie was sure about one thing – a number of people were going to be surprised when they found out her housemate dated men. Not that she'd be responsible for letting them know – Jen's secret was safe with her.

# Ch 2 – End of an Era

Savage Caverns

Careful not to get to close to the edge of the chasm, the four adventurers stared wearily at this latest obstacle. It had been a long quest and they were tired and in need of rest and sustenance.

As befitting a good leader, Alex weighed up the options. "It's too far to jump, but we have two hempen ropes and could fashion a rope ladder. With my springing boots I could leap over and fasten it for the rest of you to cross. We need to know how far it is."

Anwyn clutched his arm. "Wait. Before you use up your turn, is there anything of note on the walls?"

Smothering his delight at her perception, the storyteller chuckled. "A good question, ranger. Carved in the wall are two symbols: the first is three parallel horizontal lines."

"Air." Niamh stated – elements were her expertise.

"I always get mixed up with the wavy lines because to my mind, air's just as wavy as water and fire. I'm so glad we have you." Jinx's grin turned south as he figured the implication. "Are we supposed to fly across?"

The storyteller tutted. "The second is three capital 'M's sitting atop each other, a small distance apart."

"Like mountains. As in earth." Niamh's eyes sparkled. "What do you get by combining air and earth?" She gave the others a moment or two to work it out.

Alex leapt up. "I have it. Remember in the *Temple of Doom* when Indy threw a handful of earth into the bottomless pit and it revealed the camouflaged bridge?"

"*Last Crusade*, not *Temple of Doom*." Jinx corrected.

Rolling her eyes at the bard's pedantry, Anwyn spoke her thoughts aloud. "Air and earth is dust." She turned to Alex, encouraging. "Go for it."

After blowing on the dice, Alex threw a favourable score, and the storyteller picked up the tale.

"*Alex gathers a couple of handfuls of dirt, flinging one to reveal the edges of the stone bridge, and strides out confidently, reaching halfway before hurling the second handful as far as he can.*"

He clicked and a terrible growling assaulted their ears.

"*Echoing down the tunnels is an ominous sound.*"

"Orcs." Anwyn knew the sound well. "The basilisk's cry must have awakened them from the sleep spell."

"They are stupid creatures. I'll control the wind to blow away the dust and they won't be able to see the bridge."

"An excellent idea, Niamh, but you used your last spell slot on the sleep spell." The storyteller never wanted to make it too easy.

Anwyn checked her log. "I have a spell slot left, and I know the blast of wind spell. If I use a bonus action–"

"You haven't used one so far, so roll away." The storyteller described how, as the others hurried to safety, the ranger's spell created a gust so strong it not only blew away the dust from the bridge, all the way back to the ledge, but knocked the first half dozen orcs into a heap.

"*At the last moment, she turned and cleared the remaining dust from the path in front of her, but her intense training allowed her to run the last dozen yards without veering from the centre of the bridge.*"

*Joining her companions, they hurried through the remaining tunnels to escape the mountain and reach the river where their boat awaited."*

At the end of the campaign, as he handed out the quest medallions, distributed the booty and totted up the experience points, the storyteller felt a bigger lump in his throat than normal. He realised they'd all been so invested in these characters for so long it would be a wrench to leave them behind as they embarked on a brand new campaign with new characters. Wanting to leave them with a good feeling, he used the tried and tested epilogue technique – this wasn't the death, merely a hiatus, with the possibility of returning at a later date.

"Alex the Brave. I have enjoyed the many quests we have shared. What plans might you have in the next year?" Too late, he realised he should have asked one of the others first. Although a natural leader, the warrior rarely made a spot decision without considering all the options from every angle. He'd become better at it over the many campaigns, but something intensely personal like this, with no imminent danger or lives at stake, would have him flummoxed.

The Hermione-like twitching from Anwyn said she had absorbed the question and formulated her answer – her quick wit and razor-sharp reactions had saved the band many times in battle.

Pausing, the storyteller hoped Alex would sense her readiness and invite her to speak first. Reverting back to Isaac, he remembered a salutary lesson from his early days as DM: conflicts were always resolved more easily by standing back and giving the players a wee while to align with a task and suggest their own solution, rather than jumping in and railroading them into something which fit his world view. Sure enough, it worked as Alex spoke.

"I need a little time to ponder, would someone else like to start?"

Anwyn spoke. "I've learnt so much from all of you, and it tells me how much I still have to learn. In particular, I have little knowledge of townsfolk, and even less of city dwellers. So I shall spend some time travelling away from my beloved forests and mountains to seek out encounters in marketplaces and hostelries from here to the coast." She smiled at them. "I hope to learn to fight like Alex and maybe understand the pull of the bardic arts."

"Would you like a companion?" Jinx bowed. "I could be your guide and protector, and in return, you could teach me how to track and a little of your vast wisdom concerning the many beasts of the realm."

Niamh nodded. "I understand your impulse completely. I've been tucked away in the forests far too long and have much need of the experiences you describe."

"But I said it first." Jinx pouted. "You're merely copying me."

Alex stepped in to calm with his soothing voice. "There's no reason why you couldn't both go. A party of three is far less likely to be attacked than a lone traveller."

Anwyn peeked at him. "Would you not think to join us? We make a good team."

He glanced away, shrugging.

"Please do, Alex." Niamh touched his arm. "We all benefit from your calming presence; it brings out the best in all of us. Unless, of course, you have more pressing plans."

Another shrug. "I'd dallied with the idea of joining a force of warriors set on ridding the town of Folkesburg of their ravening horde."

"It is not far from here; we could join you." Jinx seemed overly keen.

"This all sounds encouraging. I'm glad to see your adventures may continue. But for now, I must bid you all adieu – this campaign has run its course and I wish you all well in whatever future you choose." Although the storyteller was pleased with the way things had turned out, Isaac could no longer ignore the signals from his bladder – one too many beakers of ale.

# Ch 3 – Endings & Beginnings

2019 – Season 2

After playing several campaigns in his party, no one had any doubts they'd discovered a completely different side to Isaac. He'd gradually become more of a human being, and nothing relating to the game was ever too much trouble. The four of them had become his surrogate family, and his gran fussed over them on game nights.

Although she couldn't understand the allure of playing in the gloomy cellar which ran the length of the house, she'd always have tasty snacks for them to take down, ensuring the makeshift kitchenette was stocked with tea, coffee and biscuits. Isaac filled the table-top fridge with beer, because "questing's a thirsty business, and adventurers deserve ale."

Even Rollason commented to Ben about the change in him, telling Ben to "keep up the good work."

When Ben's landlord, Oso, announced his wedding – a mere three months before the date – he and Kev were on notice to move out. Isaac's nan immediately suggested they should move into a couple of the empty rooms, naming a rent which would allow them both to start saving in earnest. It all sounded a bit too good to be true, and the main sticking point was her aversion to change – after a bad experience with students, she was adamant about them not doing anything which would make a lot of mess. They negotiated for a space to put their home gym, now an essential part of their lives. She finally agreed to let them use the garage, which meant a huge clear out. When Kev suggested they could move some of the stuff into the attic, she gave an emphatic, "No," and they never asked again.

Things fell into a comfortable rhythm as they settled into their new living arrangement, so Ben was concerned when the girls mentioned trouble with their landlord, wanting to help, but as they told the tale, he soon realised they'd got it under control.

~*~

Shortly after Georgie moved in, the third girl moved out, but the landlord couldn't find anyone to rent her bedroom, asking if they knew anyone.

Jen glanced up. "I thought you had someone coming on Friday."

He scowled. "Just another timewaster mucking me around. It's the second this week."

"The first girl had a point. It's much smaller than our rooms and you're asking the same price." Georgie was trying to be diplomatic, but Jen rarely minced words.

"Be fair – it's in a right state with the wallpaper hanging off, and it stinks of mould."

"Because you girls never have the heating on."

"Because we can't afford it with the price of everything around here. It's heat or eat."

"Feel free to move elsewhere."

"There's nowhere, the town's full during term time."

"So stop complaining or I'll put the rent up."

Georgie tried to calm things down. "We weren't complaining. If you want to get someone in, you need to do something about it. For starters, all the rooms need air bricks to ventilate them properly."

"I don't have time to do it myself, and I'm not paying the extortionate prices the cowboys charge. You two will have to pay more to make up for it."

"That's not fair."

"You've got more room, so you should pay more." He folded his arms, daring them to challenge him.

Jen's eyes narrowed. "How about if we do up the room? We'll need to use a damp sealant on the walls."

"You'd do that?" He squinted at them, suspicion writ large on his features.

"Sure. I did it for my bedroom at uni, it didn't take long at all, and it's reasonably cheap."

"I'll pay for the materials. I can get trade prices."

"So get a job lot and we'll do all three rooms." Georgie glanced at Jen and she nodded enthusiastically.

~*~

Ben grinned. "I reckon the landlord's onto a winner."

"You're not kidding." Jen winced. "A couple of decades of less-than-careful students have taken their toll on everything. The décor's tired and I've seen better furniture down the tip."

"Not forgetting the disgusting bathroom." Georgie shuddered. "Every bit of grouting is green or black."

"And the kitchen should have a health warning. I reckon by the time we've finished cleaning, renovating and decorating every room, he'll be able to charge double the rent." Jen wagged a finger. "He'd just better not try charging us."

Ben grinned, loving her quirky humour. Working closely with Jen had been a double-edged sword over the years. His burgeoning attraction had deepened as he got to know her better, but his hands were tied. He'd never date someone who worked *for* him, and would think twice before dating someone in the same company, let alone the same office. A nasty break-up with one of the sales team soured it for him. The pushy girl who'd got him in her crosshairs turned out to be a total needy nightmare. He cringed at memories of her attempt to annihilate him in front of several departmental managers in his first high-level meeting as QA rep.

Aside from the workplace restriction, he half-believed the rumours suggesting Jen didn't date men, until someone discovered the Val she talked about was a bloke. When her boyfriend turned into a fiancé, it was the kiss of death on his chances with her. *Well and truly friend-zoned.*

Until Valentine's Day. When she discovered the guy had cheated on her, he was toast – but so were all men. She kept a remote distance from them all – which was just as well because Ben had recently started seeing a girl he met on Tinder and would have been gutted at such poor timing.

Lin was sweet, but she made it clear from the start the relationship had an expiry date: she merely wanted a buddy because she found uni life so lonely. For now, it suited them both to have a friend of the opposite gender to chat and flirt with.

When Isaac's nan died in April, it hit him harder than he would ever admit and, on the face of it, he seemed to revert back to the selfish git they'd first met. For several days, Jen was the only one who could get through to him on any level. She begged the others to give him some time – after all, his nan had been his last remaining parental figure. Between them, the four friends dealt with all the necessary arrangements to ease his journey through grief.

Even Kev agreed to cut him some slack after watching him stomp off in tears five minutes into the small wake they held in the house after the funeral. He'd refused to let them seek out any of her relatives, and even Georgie respected his wishes, suggesting the rifts in the family were too deep. She created a small altar, finding pictures of Naomi and her beloved Eric when they were young and strong. Lighting the candles, she said a simple prayer that they would finally be reunited, and the others joined in.

No one felt like having a party, so they contented themselves with her favourite – a cup of tea and a slice of cake. They toasted her with a finger or two of her only vice – smooth Irish whiskey, and watched her favourite movie, *Singing in the Rain*.

On emerging from his grieving period, all Isaac wanted to do was retreat into a world where he felt safe and in control, and they humoured him, playing a session almost every evening. This led to a major sulk when Jen suggested a different venue than the cellar. Isaac refused to entertain the idea of moving from his D&D cave, claiming it was the ideal place because the dark, musty atmosphere added to the drama.

"Only if you're in an actual dungeon." Jen rarely complained, but Ben knew she hated playing there because the dank, sour smell suggested black mould, which she'd suffered from all through college.

Kev jumped in to back her up. "And none of the last few campaigns have been anywhere near a dungeon."

"Duh! How's it different to the cave in the Savage Caverns? Or the goblin emperor's mountain hall?"

Jen stood. "I'm sorry, but this place is affecting my health. I'm susceptible to damp and mould."

"You've never complained before." Isaac pouted.

"Because it's just about bearable when we're not playing so much."

Georgie stepped in to calm the rising tempers. "I haven't been up there for a while, but from what I remember, the attic is nearly as big as the cellar and it would make a stunning games room. You could have half a dozen different settings permanently set up to add a touch of realism. A cave, a forest–"

"A tavern." Kev grinned.

"Trust you to think of that first." She slapped his arm.

Isaac sighed. "I suggested something similar when I first started this party, but Nan …" He choked up.

Ben saw his concern reflected in the other's expressions. "Why don't we go up and check it out? It could be a good solution all round."

Isaac snapped into action. "Right, but I warn you, the staircase is in dire need of repair. It's proper precarious."

For once, he didn't exaggerate – halfway up, two of the stairs had rotted through completely. Several others didn't feel strong enough to withstand the weight of the girls, let alone two hulking-great body-builders. The first task was to find some suitable timber in the garage and saw off sufficient lengths for a temporary repair.

When they finally made it up to the top, Kev grumbled at the discovery the lock had rusted so badly the key refused to turn, even after a healthy squirt of WD40. "Seriously? Bloody waste of time that was. I should just kick the damned thing in. I bet it's riddled with woodworm, just like the stairs."

Georgie hovered behind him. "I wouldn't risk it. This is solid oak and–"

The loud thump and even louder curses as his boot met the unyielding wood justified her caution, even as he fell backwards, knocking her over. Luckily, Ben's quick reactions caught her, and his firm stance prevented them all from toppling like dominoes.

Amid the assorted expletives aimed in Kev's direction, Jen calmly retrieved the key and squirted another dose of the magic liquid into the keyhole. "The thing about this stuff is it's not instantaneous. The lubricant takes its own sweet time to infiltrate the glued together parts." She sprayed the key, re-inserted it and carefully twisted it clockwise and anti-clockwise, gaining a degree of movement on each manipulation. After the fifth time, they heard a tiny graunching sound as something moved, and she sprayed some more lubricant.

Ben felt the palpable tension as Kev and Isaac twitched, both obviously wanting to take over. "Leave it guys, this trap requires patient persistence, not brute force."

Jen giggled at the oft-repeated mantra from campaigns, but the distinctive click rewarded her patience as the lock finally surrendered.

"Wait." Isaac stayed her hand as it grasped the handle.

"I should go first."

Ben caught the exchange of wary glances as they pondered Isaac's motives. *What was he expecting to find?*

Kev nudged Jen. "Maybe you should add lock picking to Anwyn's skills."

Years ago, she'd have bristled at the suggestion, but she merely smiled. "What makes you think I haven't?"

"Okay, guys. It's not as bad as I imagined, but I strongly recommend you touch nothing until we have face masks. There are several decades of dust covering everything."

"So no sudden moves then." Georgie quipped.

"And absolutely no sneezing." Isaac scowled.

Kev went in next, holding the collar of his tee-shirt over his nose. "Blimey, you're not wrong. Hang on a sec – I thought dust was mostly skin cells. How can there be so much if no one's been up here for decades?"

Georgie knew. "Because this is centuries of dust, blown in from the roof as well as all the stuff which makes its way into the house on people's clothes and especially shoes. Ultimately, it all rises up to the top of the house."

"You know a lot about it."

"Had to. My little brother has a severe dust allergy which triggers his asthma. This would kill him."

"Should you be in here, then?" Kev glanced at her, his concern apparent.

"I came prepared." She donned a builder's dust mask. "I'll be fine so long as we don't start chucking it around."

"What, it's so bad you have to carry them around with you?" Kev's eyebrows wriggled in disbelief.

She rolled her eyes. "No, silly. But, you know – Isaac?

Clean freak much? I know where he keeps a stash." With a wink, she held one out to Jen. "I got one for you too."

"What a star. Ta." As Jen fitted the elastic loops over her ears, light flooded the place.

"Favouritism much? What about us lads?"

She giggled. "Real men don't wear masks."

"And Isaac?"

A snort. "He knows where they are."

Ben had found the switch and fluorescent tubes flickered and hummed, illuminating a large, rafter-clad space split into three areas by rough chipboard partitions. The first section was crammed with general family detritus – stuff people no longer used but hung onto just in case. One corner had a badly-plumbed, ancient sink unit, the tannin-stained counter cluttered with tea-making equipment including a battered kettle and some grimy mugs.

Isaac flinched. "That's new. Grampy Eric must have installed it before …"

The others shared awkward glances; he'd never said much about his granddad, let alone his parents, and the gang assumed they were all dead.

Jen nudged his arm. "It's fine if you don't want to talk."

"That's most of the problem. Nan never talked about it, and I was only eleven and in and out of hospital. At first they said he was away, hinting it was to do with his work, but I think she didn't want me to think badly of him." He glanced at Georgie. "I couldn't imagine why *your* granddad couldn't have gone instead."

~*~

Watching Isaac plying Jen with his poor-me victimy

33

expression, Georgie was thrown back to their younger selves when he would use every trick in the book to get out of doing something he didn't want to. She hadn't realised at the time, but the longer she spent with him, the more she spotted his unsubtle attempts to manipulate those around him to get his way. He perfected the art over several years of guilt-tripping all the adults in his family over his parents' poor life choices and catastrophic mistakes.

She understood Jen buying into it completely – she was, after all, the poster-girl for "soft-touch, kind-hearted and compassionate," with an outsize helping of gullible on the side. But quite why the lads tolerated his shockingly self-centred approach to everything remained one of life's great unsolved mysteries.

Having watched a couple of dozen episodes of *Big Bang Theory*, she saw the parallels between Isaac and the show's star. The way Sheldon's friends tolerated his narcissism grated so badly she could barely stand to watch it, adopting a teeth-gritting smile as people laughed out loud at his outrageous antics. *Way too close to home.*

After steering clear of Isaac for so many years, she'd been devastated to discover Jen knew him, and extremely reluctant to join the Dungeons and Dragons party. At the start, she figured maturity had softened a few edges; hoping the presence of the other three would dilute his noxious effect. *Couldn't have been more wrong if she'd tried!* After being on his best behaviour for the shortest of whiles, he was shamelessly using his nan's death as an excuse to revert to type. But what the heck was she supposed to do with the long evenings when she'd fallen out with, or otherwise alienated every other person in this area?

Returning from her musings, she noticed Isaac slinking off, leaving them to the desultory checking of the ubiquitous cardboard boxes as he wandered past the partition to the next section. *Typical!* No sign of him when there was work to be done. But she was just as invested as the others in continuing with this party, and had no problem with a bit of graft. Decorating with Jen had been fun – she loved the creativity of it.

Opening a box marked "kitchen stuff" to find a disintegrating bin-liner full of cuddly toys, she realised some of the labels couldn't be relied upon.

"Hey, you lot. Look what I've found." Isaac's excited tone suggested a far more agreeable entertainment.

They didn't need any encouragement to leave the thankless task and, as she rounded the first partition wall, Georgie stared at the structure which spanned the central section of the attic, around fifteen to twenty yards long. Also made from chipboard, it took up a third of the width. Isaac had found a hinged panel and behind it an old-style keypad was set into a smooth, white wall.

"Do you know the code?"

"I can make an educated guess." He typed in a six-digit code, but the keypad turned red.

"Wonder how many goes you get before it locks you out?" Kev did his best doom and gloom face as Ben asked why Isaac thought it was six digits.

But the second set of numbers lit up green and the door moved forward and to the side.

"How did you know that?" Ben frowned.

Georgie figured Isaac must have some prior knowledge, but his innocent expression said it was the most obvious code in the world.

"Easy. My birthday. First of March, eighty-eight."

They followed him inside to be met with the complete opposite of the dusty attic. Bright white walls gave it a futuristic, laboratory feel, and Kev remarked it looked bigger on the inside, like a Tardis. Several refrigeration cabinets with glass doors lined one wall, opposite some mobile hanging rails like they used to re-stock in clothes shops, with sealed dust covers. A long desk held two computers which Kev joked could have come from the ark.

The lads went into explorer mode, each opening a cabinet and exclaiming at the raft of ancient toys and games on the shelves with glee. Jen drifted over to a clothes rail, unzipping the cover and beckoning to Georgie. "You gotta see this, it's like proper vintage. So-oo cool."

"You mean 1970s?" Warning bells sounded as Georgie watched the boys pulling stuff off the shelves willy-nilly.

"Yeah, how did you know?"

Georgie pointed to the discreet label in a pocket on the cover, her nerves on edge as a massive crash sounded from behind her. "STOP IT RIGHT NOW, ALL OF YOU!" Her bellow made them all jump.

"What the fuck? Overkill much?" Kev seemed more rattled than the others, and she figured he was responsible for the hundreds of Lego bricks scuttling over the floor, no doubt seeking bare feet in which to embed themselves.

Scowling, she tried to explain. "Look around you; this place is set out like a museum. Everything is labelled according to the decade and you're just mixing them up."

"Your point being?" Kev winked, knowing full well how much the phrase wound her up.

"Someone worked really hard to put this all together; it wouldn't hurt you to show a bit of respect instead of acting like bulls in a china shop."

"Well whoever it was got it wrong." Isaac pulled model of Tracey Island from the top shelf of a cabinet marked 1960s and turned it over, pointing to the manufacturer's stamp. "This should be in the 1990s rack."

Ben shook his head. "Not really. Thunderbirds was originally from the sixties." He examined it with a nostalgic smile. "I remember this – they had such a run on them at Christmas in 1993 it sparked a national shortage. Blue Peter even did a special on how to make your own."

"From egg boxes and loo-roll inners? Not the same at all, mate." Kev rolled his eyes.

"I take it you were one of the lucky ones?"

"Yep. Mum waited in the queue at Toys 'R' Us. There's dedication." He smirked. "So you didn't get one, then?"

Ben shrugged. "I did actually. Mum and Dad were both big fans so they bought one earlier in the year and hid it."

"Smart."

"He didn't think so. He always regretted not buying a stack of them – reckoned he could've made a fortune."

Georgie scoffed. "Yet another example of media hype causing shortages unnecessarily. They wouldn't have been half as bad if all the papers hadn't reported about it, causing all sorts of unscrupulous types to bulk buy and make a killing. It's bloody immoral is what it is."

"What, the reporting or the dodgy entrepreneurs?" Kev used an old chestnut – he badly needed some new material.

"Both." Ignoring the wind-up, Georgie ranted on. "And social media wasn't anything like it is now – imagine if it happened today? It'd be ten times worse." She shuddered.

"So what was your shortage?" Kev winked at Ben. "Let me guess: Polly Pocket? Or was it Beanie Babies?"

She scowled. "Gender stereotype much? It was actually Buzz Lightyear."

He quirked a lip. "Apologies. I do remember – I had to wait till January."

"It was Tamagotchi for me. Don't suppose they've got one here?" Jen squealed, pouncing on the small blue device. "Oh my God, Isaac – was this yours?"

He sniffed. "Pile of junk. Bloody thing kept dying."

"Because you're supposed to take care of them and feed them and play with them to keep them alive."

"Pfft! Stupid gimmick – if I'd designed it, it would've had much more than two stupid guessing games. Couldn't even hold the attention of baby."

Shaking her head, Jen squeezed Georgie's arm. "This is raising goosebumps at all the memories. You're absolutely right, it must have taken forever to set up, we should show some respect." She nudged Kev.

He huffed a sigh. "Yeah, whatever. Some of us don't live in the past, though. And what happened to your 'live in the moment' stuff? Does the mindfulness crap go out of the window when you're faced with a bunch of old toys?"

The girls shared identical eye rolls.

"What? Now what have I said?"

"Forget it, Kev. You really don't get it, do you?"

"And probably never will." Ben retrieved the dustpan and brush he'd dumped on entering the room and bent down to sweep up the fallen bricks.

"Don't do that, you'll pick up all the dust with them."

"What dust? There isn't any."

"What? But you saw what it was like before we came in here, where's it all gone?"

"This room must be hermetically sealed, but why?" Isaac's attention was drawn to the ceiling.

Georgie noticed the place they entered bore no signs of an opening. "Hey, where did the door go?"

"That's crazy. I didn't hear it shut." Ben frowned as the others nodded their agreement. "And how's air getting in if it's sealed to prevent dust?" He peered high on the wall.

"More importantly, will it suck all the air out like the library in the Dan Brown movie about codex's?" Kev had a talent for making a drama out of a crisis.

"Surely there must be an air vent somewhere." Ben's reasonable tone took some of the panic out but, as they scoured the walls for evidence of any break in the smooth surface, anxiety snuck in and festered.

Jen had different priorities as she shuffled along the far wall, stopping at every step and peering across the room.

Georgie realised she was trying to get a fix on where they'd entered the room and joined her. "I reckon it was more to the right, directly opposite the right-hand computer." She stood in the exact spot and turned around to face the wall, running her fingers along the smooth material, probing for the slightest difference which would give away the position of the door.

"Find anything?" Ben stood behind her, echoing her moves some distance above her head. "Nothing indicates the presence of an opening."

"I know. And yet we all walked through it."

"I'm pretty sure the technology back in the late 90s wouldn't have been so sophis–"

"Hey guys, look at this." Isaac had switched on both computers, and they gathered behind the wheelie chair. "The other one is a bog-standard Hewlett Packard circa late nineties, but this has far more advanced features."

Kev picked up the mouse, affecting a broad Scottish accent. "Computer, where are we?" His mimicry of Star Trek's Scotty experiencing twentieth century technology backfired as a voice chided his lack of precision.

"Please be more specific. Do you mean which planet, country, or the address of the house?"

"Ha, that's you told." Ben held out his hand for the mouse, his grin turning cheesy as he realised he didn't need it. "Computer, how can we open the door?"

"Enter the passcode in the keypad. I cannot divulge it."

"But we can't find the keypad." Ben's instinctive response sounded like he was talking to a person, because the female voice was even more human than Siri or Alexa.

"Look harder."

Georgie definitely heard a hint of Isaac's nan in there, but before she could point this out, Jen squealed.

"It's appeared. The keypad. It definitely wasn't there earlier and it looks much more modern."

Unlike the external one, a chunky affair with discrete

keys which shouted late 90s, this was a touch pad, hidden within the door. Jen tapped 1 – 3 – 8 – 8 and stepped back as a slice of wall moved soundlessly toward her then glided to the side, revealing the dusty attic beyond.

"Move quickly. You have thirty-three seconds before the door seals and all the air will be evacuated from the chamber." The computer's warning became more urgent. "The five of you will have only three minutes of oxygen."

Kev didn't hesitate, diving out and tugging Georgie with him, but Isaac scurried back to the desk.

# Ch 4 – Dust and Floods

May 2019 – Season 2

The door began closing as Jen went through, and Ben barely pulled Isaac through in time, nagging at him. "What was so important you had to risk your life?"

"My notebook." He pocketed it, his face wobbling.

Kev huffed a noisy breath. "Now I really do feel like I'm in a Dan Brown novel. Scary, much?"

Everyone spoke at once – they all had dozens of questions about what they'd just experienced, but Isaac ignored them all as he punched in the entry code. The keypad lit up red and a scrolling LCD display informed he only had two more attempts. "What? That can't be right." He jabbed a finger toward the one.

Jen's quick reflexes caught his hand. "Stop. Do you want to lock us out indefinitely? Did you not hear the 'evacuating the air' warning? She's hardly going to allow the door to open while that's going on, is she?"

"S'pose not. You know it's not a woman, don't you?"

"Of course. But it doesn't hurt to personify her."

He snorted. "So when can we try again?"

"Patience, dear boy." Kev did a mean imitation of Isaac's nan, causing a dirty look.

Ben picked up on the fun. "What, you think he's grown some tolerance in the past hour? Surely you know his body rejects the concept, let alone his mind."

"True. I had forgotten. But I get the impression the chamber doesn't approve of dust-making machines in its pristine space."

"You mean humans?" Jen grinned.

"Exactly. It may take a full 24 hours to recover."

"And it's much more of a capsule than a chamber." Ben winked.

"A time capsule. See what you did there. But what do we do in the meantime?" Isaac pouted.

"It wouldn't hurt to make a start on getting the rest of the attic as dust-free as possible." Jen gestured at the room.

Ben grinned. "Might make her friendlier towards us."

"Don't be ridiculous. You're still talking as though it's a living entity."

"Your problem being?" Ben's hands rested on his hips.

"For gods' sake." Isaac scoffed. "It's called science fiction for a reason, you know. Emphasis on the fiction."

Kev nudged Ben. "That's my line, don't wear it out."

Isaac sniffed. "I think you'll find *I* actually used the phrase – or a version of it – long before either of you."

"Whatever, it's so-oo last decade." Jen rolled her eyes. "And just a stalling tactic. Now grab a box and get sorting."

"But Isaac said to touch nothing until we have face masks." Kev's grin challenged.

"Only if you need one. Big strong lad like you afraid of a bit of dust? There's one under the sink if you need it."

"I don't know why we'd even bother. Just hire a skip and dump the lot." Kev held up his hands as both girls glared. "At least, it's what I'd do if it were up to me."

"Thankfully, it's not." Georgie folded her arms.

"But it *is* up to me and I thoroughly agree." Isaac gestured at it. "It's just old junk nobody wants."

Georgie rounded on the pair of them. "You may not

want it, but there's plenty of less well-off people who'd be thrilled to buy some of this stuff from a charity shop."

"Here we go. Georgie's got her reuse, recycle head on."

"It's the only head I have. Unlike some, I care about the planet and the effect of the modern, throwaway society."

"All right, Greta." Kev smirked. "If you want to waste weeks of your life sorting old tat to appease your social conscience, go ahead. Just don't expect us to give up valuable time we could spend on something useful."

"Like what? Gaining another level in one of your stupid strategy games? Or amassing an even bigger virtual treasure hoard?"

"Or is it pretending to steal a few more cars?" Jen's attempt to support Georgie backfired as Kev scoffed.

"You've never even played grand theft auto – I don't know why you always harp on about it."

"Because it's immoral and teaches young lads all the wrong values."

"All right, mum. Keep your curlers in." He nudged Ben's arm, suggesting a session of the latest multi-player role game they were into.

"Actually, I'll stay here and help the girls."

"Get you, Mr Suck-up."

"The sooner we get this lot cleared, the sooner we can move the D&D up here. And if we damp-proofed the cellar it would make a great gym." Ben's pointed glare bounced off Kev's total indifference.

"Well good luck with that. Are you coming, Isaac?"

"Yeah, we'll come back tomorrow and try again."

With the negative energy elsewhere, the other three had

a much more pleasant time. Ben didn't rate his usefulness when it came to sorting stuff, and figured his first task should be to provide tea and biscuits for the workers.

He returned with the vacuum cleaner to do battle with the layers of dust. After emptying the bag for the fifth time, he reasoned the machine could make no further impression until they got rid of all the dust-filled stuff. He pointed to the roof. "We'll need to seal the underside of the tiles in the rafters ASAP or it'll be just as bad in a couple of weeks."

"Hardly weeks." Georgie chuckled. "Months maybe."

As they high-fived, Jen glanced away, unsure why she should feel so disturbed by their easy camaraderie. As ever, she resorted to physical activity to divert her mind, quickly getting into a rhythm. She found a bunch of labels on the floor where they'd fallen when the glue had dried, and soon figured there was actually a method to how the boxes were stored. Nipping downstairs, she found a couple of thick black marker pens, so they could re-label.

By the end of the afternoon, they'd stacked up a bunch of boxes by the door which could go straight to the charity shop, based on Isaac's lack of interest in anything he considered boring old junk.

The following day, they went up straight after breakfast, hoping to spend some more time exploring their new toy, and Isaac suggested they shouldn't wear the same clothes as yesterday as those would be full of dust. But he hadn't thought it through and they'd been in there less than five minutes when the computer shooed them out, saying the dust levels had reached a critical level. A red strobe light twirled and an alarm had them dashing out pronto.

"Of course that's down to you lot raising all the dust yesterday – it's probably suspended in the air at ten times the level it was yesterday." Isaac grumped. "Now we have to wait another twenty-four hours before we can try again."

"All the more reason to clear it out. We should get rid of as much as we can in the meantime." Jen had brought up some disposable gloves because her hands had dried out yesterday.

"Good luck with that." Kev winked. "Wanna try level twelve, Isaac?"

But his attention was buried in a box filled with old comic books. "So *that's* where these went. I thought I'd lost them – even re-bought some of them."

"I spotted another half-dozen boxes, but some of them show signs of damp so they may have gone mouldy." Georgie pointed at a stack. "Why don't you two take them down to the garage and sort through them there? Then you won't be sending fungus spores into the attic."

This task caught Kev's imagination and the pair made several three-storey journeys laden with boxes. As they collected the last load, Isaac stressed they'd take any more comics the others found, just to leave them by the door.

The girls discovered a stack of old bedding in bin liners. All the old blankets and candlewick bedspreads needed airing to remove the storage smell before they could go in the recycling bins, along with a pile of old coats. Georgie suggested they hung onto the sheets to use during decorating, but the old, yellowing duvets and pillows could go to the animal shelter. They built up various piles for distribution, the tip being the smallest as they found creative ways to recycle.

Meanwhile, Ben darted around measuring various dimensions, which he marked on a rough sketch of the roof space. Interrogating several sites, he soon got an idea of the necessary materials required to do a proper cladding job. Having calculated the quantities, he costed it all out, coming up with a top line which was a fraction of what the professionals quoted.

"Because the biggest cost is the labour. Sounds like a lot of man-hours." Jen never saw the point in pratting about with gender-based nouns.

"If we all pitched in to help, it's entirely doable." Georgie examined the sketch.

Ben voiced his concern about his lack of DIY expertise. "And I've done far more than the other two put together, so I'm guessing they're not exactly gonna volunteer."

Over dinner, they broached the subject and Kev reacted predictably, with a stack of justifications for his inability to help. "I'm not creative like you girls, I'll muck things up."

Jen recognised his fear of failure kicking in. "For goodness' sake, it's not rocket science, just a matter of applied maths."

"It's easy for you to say, you're used to helping your mum, but I was never allowed to. I just wrecked stuff because I was so clumsy. And still am."

"It's a skill like everything else. The more you do, the better you'll get." Georgie tried to reassure.

"But I'm a big-picture person; I don't do details. You need to have patience for all the fiddly bits."

"That's me out, then. I couldn't be bothered to wait in the queue when they handed out patience." Isaac sniggered.

Jen's hard stare matched her relentless tone. "So you leave the finicky stuff to us and you guys can do the heavy lifting – you'll be the muscle."

By dint of persuasion, ego-stroking and outright blackmail, they got the reluctant twosome to agree to spend the following day – a bank holiday – up there.

This time, when they tried, the capsule wouldn't even open, and the scrolling message read "Dust alert."

Jen wasn't the only one to notice Isaac's U-turn. Instead of pouting and making excuses, he drove them hard, and Kev grumbled about being a pack horse. Ben suggested they go to the DIY store to pick up the materials.

"What a Moaning Minnie." Isaac scorned as they left. "Afraid of a bit of hard work."

"Hardly. We've been at it for hours. We should take a break and make some lunch."

"No, it'll take too long. I'll order something in so we don't have to stop and make it."

"Have you thought maybe we want to have a break?"

"Yeah, sure. But this way we don't have to get changed and there'll be no clearing up afterwards. Much more efficient."

"Just make sure there's plenty of cold beer in the fridge – this dust chokes."

"Only one can each until we finish, then you can get pooh-faced if you want."

Georgie giggled. "I think you mean shit-faced."

Isaac's face came over all lemon-sucky. "That might be

a term you feel comfortable with, but Nan never allowed swearing, and was particularly averse to scatology."

The girls exchanged a glance; the old-fashioned, courtly manner was without doubt his most endearing trait.

Jen suspected he knew more than he was letting on about things when he suggested they waited a while before trying the code again, but she didn't call him on it. As far as she was concerned, their efforts in reducing the dust could be nothing but beneficial for all as they seemed destined to spend a good deal of time up there.

The final section, on the other side of the time capsule, contained a cornucopia of unlikely treasures, from an old-fashioned dressmaker's dummy to authentic Victorian toys, including a rocking horse and doll's house. Both considerably larger than modern versions, they needed a little TLC but were otherwise intact.

"Wow. Give these a coat of paint and they'd fetch a pretty penny or two." Ben seemed particularly impressed by the doll's house, rubbing at layers of grime to reveal terracotta roof tiles and a pastel-blue front door.

Examining his find, Jen's eyes shone. "Sounds like fun. I love restoring stuff to its original beauty."

Georgie went straight for the furniture. "Talking of beauty, look at the inlays on this wardrobe."

Jen studied them. "They're gorgeous. What wood is it?"

"Walnut." Georgie ran her hand over it. "I reckon these are the real deal, Isaac. They could be worth a lot."

Kev's ears pricked up. "Shouldn't need much tarting up to fetch a tidy profit. If Ben gets the toys, I'll have these."

Georgie scowled at him before addressing Isaac.

"Actually, I reckon you should do up a couple of bedrooms with all the antiques, they'll make fabulous guest rooms."

Jen backed her up, squeezing Isaac's arm. "Yep. It'd be much better than the awful cheap stuff in most of the rooms at the moment."

He grunted. "Because Nan had to let out some of the rooms after Grampy Eric left." His lip trembled. "They didn't take care of the furniture, so it ended up here."

"Hey, it could be the way forward. Fill all those empty bedrooms with lodgers. "

"Having students in?" He shuddered. "A bunch of smelly, noisy plebs turning the kitchen into a grease factory and growing pot on the windowsills. I don't think so."

Ben tutted. "They're not all like that. We'd help you screen them, and their rent would help pay for the upkeep and council tax – it must be massive."

Isaac didn't seem at all keen on the idea, suggesting they limited their energies, prioritising sealing the rafters, starting with the first section. Meanwhile, he got various workmen in to install cubicles for a toilet and shower and plumb in a proper sink unit for a small kitchenette. He had a stack of annual leave, so he used some of it to be a demanding, hands-on project manager.

This of course raised a lot more dust so Ben waited until they were done to have another go with the vacuum cleaner, but it was a task of diminishing returns as each use resulted in a mist of particles. A while after he switched it off, they floated down to settle as a layer of fine dust. His solution involved a couple of dampened microfibre cloths.

Georgie shook her head. "Blimey, mate. You turn

everything into a science project."

"Hangover from Mum. 'If a thing's worth doing–"

"It's worth doing well." The girls chorused.

By the end of the second week, the entire attic space had been transformed into a "clean room" almost worthy of an operating theatre. All the items capable of shedding dust had been shifted to either a spare bedroom, the garage for processing, or off the premises altogether – destination a charity shop or the local tip. Only the floor remained, and they were checking out various options including thermal-backed raised boarding.

Isaac's enthusiasm to get back into the capsule knew no bounds – he even persuaded them to take a day off work on the Friday to assemble the units for the kitchenette and clean the grout off the tiles in the loo and shower room. By the afternoon, they were ready for their third foray into the time capsule, and all gave a cheer when the door slid open.

This time, he got the computer to explain the rules: the system monitored the density of dust particles and, when it reached a critical level, they got a ten-minute, and then a three-minute warning before safety measures were enabled.

"Computer, display this data so we can analyse it."

A thermometer-style graphic appeared on the screen of the other computer, showing it was already at 26%.

"Why is it still so high?"

"All our clothes contain contaminants, particularly shoes and outer layers. From now on, we wear hotel slippers – I found a drawer full of unopened ones. And we should use those paper overalls they wear at crime scenes.

Maybe we need a decontamination airlock."

Kev frowned. "Overkill much?"

"Computer, how long till we reach critical level?"

"Approximately twenty minutes."

"Thank you." Ben couldn't help his natural manners. "Right, I suggest the four of us focus on trying to make sense of the clothes and artefacts while Isaac interrogates the computer. Get to it."

After sorting through three racks of clothes, Jen had no clue why they deserved a place in this strange collection. There didn't seem to be any rhyme or reason to the items, they were all shapes and sizes in many disparate styles.

Kev could think of only one aspect. "If you ever decided to get rid, you'd make a killing on Vinted."

"What are you like?" Jen shook her head. "I'll tell you what though, if anyone wanted to make a bit of money on the side, I bet there's dozens of am-dram clubs who'd be thrilled to hire the whole rack for a period piece."

"Never mind am-dram, the regional theatres would be interested." Georgie brandished lime green hot-pants.

After comparing notes, it was clear that, like the toys, games and artefacts in the racks, the clothes were limited to the five decades of the fifties through to the nineties.

When they emerged, Ben slid Isaac a glance. "Surely Eric's notebook had some kind of instructions about the purpose of that thing." The ruse worked.

"Not at all, just various designs for the capsule and the dust-filtration system." Isaac glanced away, obviously miffed at being caught out. "Oh, and some lists at the back with the prices of things – he was fascinated by such stuff."

52

"So you think it's just some kind of museum then?"

"Probably. You didn't really believe it was a time capsule, did you?" Isaac smirked. "You do *know* time-travel isn't possible, don't you?"

"Psh. Of course I do. But I'd like to have a peek – I'm quite interested, too."

"Sure. Not a problem. But I warn you, most of it's in code – quite a complex layered one."

Ben damped down his excitement. "Why encode if it wasn't important?"

Isaac played it down. "I reckon it's just something he was thinking of patenting. He was a bit paranoid about his inventions."

"We could all work on it together – we're not without skills in that area."

"Of course. That would be great."

"And a proper snoop around those computers – the evacuation system looks quite complicated."

"That's doable too, although you wouldn't get long because by the time they've taken forever to boot up, you'll only have ten minutes before the dust-bot boots you out." He chortled at his own wit, and Ben couldn't help thinking he was over-playing it.

The following morning, something dripped on Ben's head and he woke to find wet patches on his bed. As he examined the ceiling, a shout from the next room said Kev was also getting rained on.

"What the fuck? Isaac, there's been a leak. A pipe must have burst or something."

A loud crash had them both dashing into his room where a chunk of plaster had fallen on his bed and water poured through.

Ben reacted first. "Where's the stop cock?"

"What do you mean?"

"The main – never mind. Shove your bed out of the way before it soaks through to the mattress. Kev, go and check the airing cupboard, I'll check under the kitchen sink." He dashed down and found the shutoff valve, turning the red wheel until no more water flowed into the kitchen sink. When he returned, Isaac was throwing all his most precious items into a suitcase.

"Have you phoned the plumber?"

"I don't know any. Nan always dealt with the tradesmen."

"She must have kept a list – they're like gold dust. Never mind, I'll sort it." Trying to get anyone out on a Sunday was a challenge, but he figured Isaac could afford the exorbitant call out, and he and Kev could chip in for the repairs. By the time the guy arrived, they'd helped Isaac clear everything into his nan's old room, and moved all their stuff into the two rooms at the other end to the damaged ones.

The plumber knew a builder who could repair the leaking ceilings, suggesting they used fans to get the air moving and a dehumidifier for Isaac's room. He assured them nothing they'd done in the attic could have caused the leak, just old pipes, and gave a reasonable quote to replace the entire system.

When the girls came round, Isaac presented the idea of

converting the second floor into six similar suites, themed for a different decade from the 50s to the 00s. He claimed to have been inspired the experience of transforming the attic, and when they sketched out a few ideas, the girls proposed a minor change, with the last suite having two guest rooms filled with the antique furniture.

With a surprising business head, Isaac hired an architect to re-design the space, and a team of builders spent months making structural changes to turn the 70s behemoth into a carbon-neutral, eco-friendly des-res any TV restoration designer would be proud of. Living amid the turmoil was challenging, and they helped Isaac move his bed up to the attic to avoid the worst of the dust and upheaval for the duration, and the extra shower room was invaluable.

Ben and Kev stayed put while the builders gutted the rest of the floor, moving to the opposite end when the rooms were ready. Their old rooms were converted into Isaac's luxury pad with a sunken bath in the ensuite.

When the crew finished, the walls were white-painted plaster – a blank canvas ready for turning into something glorious. The friends agreed to kit out a suite each, and Ben opted to take over the 70s unit. Having grown up with his mum's obsession for the music of the decade, he spent many a happy hour trawling the internet for authentic artefacts. He kept most of the walls a neutral beige and limited the "groovy" brown, turquoise and orange to a feature wall and various accents. Not that he was fussed, but he didn't want to offend the delicate sensibilities of anyone he invited to stay in the room.

*Chance would be a fine thing.*

Georgie did something similar with the sixties suite, with classic Andy Warhol prints vying with the spectacular Indian wall hangings. She'd gone for broke in the bathroom, which gave a truly psychedelic experience, complete with copious candles and incense. Jen did the 50s room in two halves – black and white film noir versus the bright rock and roll colours.

Just like the 80s, Kev's room had all the poor style excesses and wall-to-wall retro gadgets. However Ben couldn't help but notice how both he and Isaac relied on the girls – especially Jen – to help with their stylistic decisions. As the pair of them competed for Jen's attention, Georgie's frequent eye rolls said she'd noticed it too.

By the end of the year, Isaac, Ben and Kev had fabulous rooms worthy of a classy London hotel with en-suite, kitchenette and air-con. Apart from the cellar gym, the real pull was the high-tech, sound-proofed games room with a bank of monitors where they could play the most demanding of multi-player role games amid a to-die-for sound system.

# Ch 5 – The Plague

2020/1 – Season 3

Twenty-twenty brought with it a global pandemic which had everything shutting down. During March, media across the world did their best to create countrywide shortages by focussing on shelves empty of loo rolls, hand wash and basic food staples.

Kev returned from an expedition to the supermarket full of disgust. "It's totally bonkers. I heard one old woman telling her friend she'd been shopping every day this week and now her cupboards are bulging and she has nowhere else to store it. But she *still* had a half-full trolley. Bloody ridiculous."

Jen winced at his vehemence. "It's just fear. You never know, she could have lived through post-war rationing."

"It's no excuse. People like her are the ones causing the shortages. If they only bought what they needed, there'd be enough for everyone."

"Oh dear." Jen frowned. "I feel bad, because I bought a couple of packs of speciality mixes for Isaac's bread-maker. I figured it would help if we could make our own."

"Don't feel bad – I had the same idea and asked Kev to get some yeast and bread flours." Ben stacked the packs on the counter. "But nothing like this much. I reckon you've gone well OTT."

Jen tutted. "Talk about pots and kettles."

"What?" Kev had the grace to squirm. "You said to get a couple of yeasts and some different flavours, so I did."

"Can't imagine Isaac as our baker – the novelty wore

off before the Christmas decorations were down."

Ben grinned at Jen's quip. "He's the very definition of short attention span. But I quite fancy having a go. Did you get the olives? I found a recipe for olive bread which sounds yummy." From then on, the house filled with the mouth-watering smell of freshly baked bread several times a week as Ben experimented with exotic recipes for tomato, onion and cheese breads.

The full lockdown came in at the end of March, but they had no need to furlough as the company had figured out how to connect everyone remotely to the relevant aps they needed for their job. Jen virtually lived there from Monday to Friday, and having four of them in one house was a real benefit, although Isaac stayed mostly in his room rather than use the shared study. Georgie's job was deemed non-essential and even with the partial furlough she found it difficult to make ends meet. Shortly after, the girls' landlord decided he needed their house for some needy relatives, and it was a blessing in disguise as Isaac invited them to take over the suites they'd decorated.

When Kev found out the girls had barely watched any of the last season of *Big Bang Theory*, he declared this the perfect opportunity to get them on board.

Ben looked up. "I could go for that. I missed a couple of episodes and always meant to go back to fill in the gaps."

Jen shrugged. "It's an easy watch – I love the smart humour."

"Not to mention the way Penny's so much braver than all the boys." Kev scoffed.

"Hey maybe we should watch them all from the

beginning." Isaac glanced around.

"Good idea. It's ages since I saw the old ones."

"It would take months." Georgie pulled a face.

"Over a hundred hours. Around eight hours per season."

"Only you would know that, Kev. But three episodes is only an hour, we could do a season in a week." Jen glanced hopefully at Georgie, who raised capitulating hands.

"Is season eleven where Sheldon marries Amy? There's some good episodes with her hen do and that ridiculous wedding dress."

"The actual wedding is the first in season twelve, but there's a stack of preparation ones in eleven." Kev was more than a tad obsessed with the show, fiddling on his phone. "We should all pick an episode from the previous one and watch it first. I liked the one where they were trying to decide who should be best man and maid of honour."

The credits rolling for the final one in the last season immediately jumped to the very first episode, and they fell down the inevitable rabbit hole. Jen could have put money on Kev making the inevitable joke about painting the Forth bridge, cringing when he had to tell Georgie it took so long to paint, as soon as they got to one end, they had to start from the beginning. He gave a slight scoff. "I can't believe you've not heard about it."

She winked. "I have, I just love it when you mansplain."

In mid-April, the lockdown was extended by at least three weeks, but the media speculated it could be June before restrictions were lifted. Isaac's germaphobia had him returning to the attic room, his only contact with the outside world via electronic devices. He had everything he needed to survive on microwaved meals and the fresh fruit Jen left outside the door. She worried about his lack of fresh air and exercise, but nothing would convince him to emerge from his sanctuary.

With daily walks and weekly food deliveries from local supermarkets, the others coped a lot better, but the hardest bit was staying positive. Normally, they'd have appreciated the opportunity to indulge in wall-to-wall D&D campaigns, but Isaac refused to let them into the attic. They tried a couple of sessions with him running it over various group chats, but it didn't work well because the apps were all overloaded due to insane demands from everyone trying to communicate virtually. No matter what time of the evening or weekend they tried, technological shortcomings ruined the experience, and they gave it up as a bad job.

Appointing himself entertainments manager, Kev suggested themed weeks devoted to their favourite movie franchises, starting with *Indiana Jones* and *Die Hard*. Every evening, they watched a couple of the movies, and on Saturday had a Christmas-themed party where people vied to wear the most outrageous jumper.

The following week was *Harry Potter*, including *Fantastic Beasts*, and they watched three movies on some evenings to fit them in. The turkey and stuffing rolls and souped-up Brussel sprouts were replaced with all their favourite foods from the school canteens. Kev had really gone to town with the décor, laying out a couple of candelabra on a trestle table so it looked like the great hall at Hogwarts.

After a while, they stopped inviting Isaac as his response always involved quoting the latest deaths along with all the scaremongering rife on social media. Jen knew he'd got it bad when he refused to come down for the Tolkien week when they watched all six *Hobbit* and *Lord of the Rings* movies – over seventeen hours' worth.

As weeks turned to months, they settled into the peculiar limbo: contact with families reduced to twice weekly phone calls where everyone had very little news except to report they'd managed to avoid the plague.

With scant opportunity for exotic themed food, the end-of-week feast became a general party spread where each person provided a couple of their favourite dishes and they all shared. Jen provided homemade coleslaw, pasta salad and green salad, along with herby chicken pieces. Georgie batch-baked awesome veggie dishes – curries, quiches and to-die-for halloumi and onion pasties.

Ben's contribution centred on fresh bread, dough balls or pizza bases along with a selection of spicy Indian or Chinese nibbles such as samosas or pancake rolls. Kev made potato wedges and always had several different cheeses in the fridge, along with half-a-dozen pickles, so the meals invariably ended with cheese and biscuits.

Although it seemed a little indulgent to have a party every week, Jen couldn't help agreeing with Kev about the importance of keeping up morale. The diet of house arrest, wall-to-wall bad news and fear-mongering statistics took a toll on everyone's mental health.

When Kev announced a choice between superheroes or

time-travel, they voted for the latter. He'd combined the *Back to the Future* and *Terminator* franchises and the girls immediately thought of raiding the clothes in the attic for suitable outfits, but first they had to get past the gatekeeper.

Jen volunteered, knocking the door as he'd arranged before video calling on WhatsApp. His skin looked even paler than normal, with dark bags under his eyes.

"What is it?" The irritation was definitely more marked than normal. "I don't care about your theme. I can watch whatever I want, when *I* want to."

She tried to get the right amount of concern in her voice: too much had him grousing about not being a child, and not enough made him sulk because nobody cared about him. "I'd like to come in the attic."

"You know the rule – have you had a test?"

"You can only have a test if you have symptoms, and I don't have any."

"When was the last time you were in contact with anyone outside the house?"

"A fortnight ago when I went shopping."

"What about the others?"

"Longer. And they have no symptoms either."

He snorted. "Take your temperature and show me."

He'd organised a sanitisation station outside the door with a digital thermometer, and she pointed it at her forehead, showing him the result.

"Remember to sanitise it before you replace it. Why do you want to come in? I left my laundry yesterday; if it's done you can leave it in the basket for a week as usual."

When she explained about wanting to borrow some of

the vintage clothes for their party he just said no and disconnected the call.

The others had been waiting out of sight and Kev scoffed. "I expected nothing less. We should just unlock the door and get what we need."

Ben frowned. "Strong-arming isn't the best tactic."

"It worked before."

A flashback to Elf-height-gate had Jen cringing at her part in condoning Kev's outrageous intimidation tactic by her lack of inaction. At the time, she'd been too fired with righteous indignation at Isaac's arrogance in distancing himself from a problem he'd created. But it had haunted her in several quiet moments, breaking into her meditations and filling her with guilt. Although it was too late to take it back, she could at least prevent a recurrence of the violence, particularly when he was so vulnerable.

She put her hand on Kev's arm. "Only because he knew he was in the wrong. I wouldn't feel right about bullying our way in and taking the stuff against his will. He has every right to refuse."

Georgie snorted. "Leave it with me." Phone in hand, she scampered down the stairs, returning after a short while with his instructions about how it would work.

Minutes later, clad in masks and suitably sanitised, they were in Kev's "air-lock" shelter shrugging on the white overalls, while Isaac opened the time capsule. He kept his distance inside, monitoring the readouts and nagging them to hurry up and choose.

As the others left, Jen approached Isaac, noting the way his eyes widened and his whole body tensed. "Listen. I'm worried about the effect being cooped up in here alone is having on you."

"I'm perfectly fine. I've been exercising every few days–"

"We can hear you, and it rarely lasts more than ten minutes. It's nothing like enough."

He bristled. "It's better than nothing."

"True. But you need to do stretches and load-bearing–"

"Those two have you brainwashed."

She ignored the accusation. "–and more than anything you need fresh air and sunlight to regulate your metabolism and circadian rhythms. You're obviously not sleeping well – just twenty minutes in the garden every morning getting the sun in your eyes will help no end."

"I can just stand in front of the skylight."

"Not the same. You need to breathe in fresh air."

"Next you'll have me hugging trees like Georgie."

Jen knew better than to launch into the benefits of walking in woods. "It wouldn't hurt to hug anything once in a while. If you hug someone for twenty seconds it releases oxytocin which boosts the immune system."

"And combats the stress hormone, cortisol. I know the science, doctor Jen."

She sighed. "I know you're like Sheldon about physical contact, but can I suggest you at least spend some time in the garden every day? If you let us know when you're going, we'll give you a clear path to the back door."

"You can suggest anything you like. I don't intend to put myself at risk of catching this lurgy."

"How is it a risk? None of us have it and they reckon

64

it's not spreading more than two metres."

He scoffed. "They don't know anything like enough about it to make accurate recommendations."

"At least consider it. If you don't develop symptoms in the next few days–"

"The incubation can be up to twelve days."

"In extreme cases. The average is a week. Anyway, the point is, you need to stop holing yourself up here – it's not good for you. As soon as you feel able, get outside."

When they got back down, Kev nudged Georgie. "What did you say to him? I really can't imagine."

"I just asked what Naomi would say if she knew."

"Ha – using his me-maw against him. Classic!"

In the end, no doubt due to terrifying himself with all the scary stuff on the net about people's physical and mental health suffering, he capitulated, starting off with a solo walk outside. After a couple of symptom-free weeks, he gradually integrated back in, joining in the *Stranger Things* binge-fest, which lasted two weeks. It ended with them playing the show's associated D&D game based on Will's campaign which someone had bought Georgie for her birthday long before Covid, still wrapped in sealed polythene. He bridled at the lack of meat at the feast, adding Kentucky fried chicken, sausages and pork pie.

Isaac wanted to do some of the *Star Trek* series, but they didn't get many votes, so he settled for *Firefly*, including the spin-off movie, *Serenity*. Next came *Agent Carter*, followed by a *Marvel* marathon which included several spin-off series and lasted months.

By the end, the novelty of wall-to-wall binging had

worn off although it had become the hardest of habits to break. Despite loving each of the different shows, Jen found herself wishing she could escape the dreadful inertia which held her in its thrall every night as they hit the "next episode" and "skip credits" time after time until their eyelids drooped.

When the government finally began easing restrictions, Gaming UK took a sensible stance, allowing people to remain working from home, and Kev remarked cynically they were probably saving a minor fortune on power bills, so it was in their interest.

As people took tentative steps to meet up with their estranged families, the government delighted in releasing almost daily rules and regulations.

Kev's parents were the most vociferous against these, and he echoed their sentiments. "For frick's sake – who do they imagine they are? Telling us we're allowed to leave our homes as long as we don't stay overnight anywhere apart from our designated home."

"Been talking to your dad again?" Ben rolled his eyes.

"He's right. How the heck are they gonna police it? And the whole 'gatherings of more than six people not allowed outdoors' and not allowed at all indoors, is total crap. It means if mum and dad wanted to visit they couldn't because there are already five people in the house."

"They could, because we wouldn't all come out."

"Yeah, but who wants to stand out in the garden when it's pouring with rain?"

"May I remind you it's summer?" Ben grinned.

"You are aware this is England?" Jen winked. "Summer means a couple of dry days in August if you're lucky."

Kev was too busy ranting to bite. "And all this crap about support bubbles – nothing's gonna stop mum from seeing her dad – he's in his eighties and lives alone."

"Which is the whole reason behind support bubbles."

Each new pronouncement caused a fresh outburst from Kev, but when he returned from visiting his folks, his conspiracy-theory outbursts mysteriously stopped and he took a back seat, not challenging anything the others said about any aspect of the pandemic, even when the mask debate hit new levels of nonsense.

Various incentives to aid the ailing hospitality industry, such as "Eat out to help out," fell flat as too many people lived in media-driven terror of catching the disease. The wedding industry was hardest hit as the restriction of wedding receptions to thirty people led many "save the dates" in people's diaries to be indefinitely postponed.

September saw a ten pm curfew hitting all forms of hospitality along with a return to working from home for those who'd ventured back to their offices. Halloween tricksters couldn't have predicted the ultimate scare – a second lockdown from November fifth putting the kybosh on several bonfire night celebrations.

When the lockdown ended four weeks later, the strict three-tier measures – affectionately known as Plan B – to slow spread of a new, more virulent variant impressed nobody. The ensuing debate about exactly who could be meeting who over the Christmas period resulted in several shenanigans as people tried to figure out combinations of family groupings which wouldn't break the rules about up to three households meeting in any one venue.

When a fourth tier was introduced at the winter solstice, certain pundits saw the writing on the walls, and the announcement about Christmas rules tightening even further to allow a maximum of six people on the 25th saw even the most ardent rule-followers leaning toward anarchy. Many families protested at the arbitrary limit, sneaking in a seventh or eighth family member rather than leaving someone on their own.

The New Year had more areas entering tier four and warnings of even tougher restrictions for children returning to school. January saw the third national lockdown days after the first person received the Oxford–AstraZeneca COVID-19 vaccine. The three primary companies racing for the accolade of being first now fought to have the most viable, reliable and safest solution. The short shelf-life – a matter of hours in one case – brought the potential for huge waste. And that was before the awful allergic reactions had those in need of an epi-pen dropping like flies.

As usual, Kev came down on the side of the conspiracy theorists, arguing "Big Pharma" hadn't had anything like enough time to test it properly and could know nothing about the long-term effects.

Isaac scathingly pointed out their cynical strategy of using septuagenarians and people in care homes as guinea pigs meant they'd have sufficient failure data by the time they offered it to people in their prime.

Public pressure forced the beleaguered Boris Johnson to release his roadmap for lifting lockdown, and as they gathered around the TV for the latest pronouncement, Georgie noted he'd chosen an auspicious date – the twenty second of February.

"I give up. What's so special about it? If it had been this time next year, it would have been a perfect palindrome." Isaac's scorn challenged them to explain.

Kev wrote it down in figures: 22/02/2021 "Ha – you mean it would read the same forwards and backwards."

"It is what a palindrome *normally* means. So–"

Everyone shushed him as the PM described the plan as "cautious but irreversible, led by data not dates," stressing it was subject to certain conditions being met, including tests on new variants, vaccines and infection rates, with all restrictions ending by 21st June.

"An even more startling choice, being midsummer. Who knew he had pagan tendencies?" Kev chuckled.

Isaac turned to Georgie. "Well come on, why is today's date auspicious?"

"Any number with a multiple of eleven has powerful magic, and twenty-two is strong, but thirty-three is even stronger with the power of three as well as eleven."

"So my birthday this year should be extra special because I'll be thirty three?" Isaac's smirk said not.

"In theory, yes. And if you add all the digits together–"

"So, five twos and a one, which is also eleven, making it doubly magical." Kev's wink said he didn't believe either – he merely wanted to show off how fast he could add.

During March, vaccines were rolled out to sixty-year-olds, with roughly a third of the population rushing to take up this "lifeline." But the real freedom came in April when the lateral flow tests were made freely available to everyone, because now people had "proof" they were not infected. In the end, many of the proposed dates got moved out and it was actually the nineteenth of July before the final stage of COVID restrictions were lifted in England, abolishing social distancing rules.

Eventually, things returned to a semblance of the former freedoms people called "the new normal."

2022 – Season 4

After a couple of years in the grip of the worldwide pandemic, the media's attempts in February to scare people into staying at home with red weather alerts from storm Eunice fell on deaf ears. Eager to prolong the doom and gloom, the press tried to vilify the latest variant, Omicron. But it seemed the intelligent virus had mutated into a form which no longer killed its host, presumably so it could spread further and faster.

The Tik-Tok twitterati tried to inject a measure of hope with uplifting, spiritual messages about the powerful manifestation energy of the master number 22.

Isaac commented that the triple appearance in 22/02/2022 only worked if written in the British form with the day first. The waterfall of optimism about the future was short lived and a couple of months later, Kev was back on his conspiracy theory soap box.

"So it's another palindrome: 22/4/22, and what have we had so far this year? Storms of Biblical proportions, a media feeding frenzy over rule-breaking social meetings in government, and a power-hungry Bolshevik turning us all into paupers."

"So, floods, Partygate and the onset of world war three. And we all thought we'd get a break after the pandemic."

"No such luck. The press are in their element – they've never had so much click-bait fodder and they get almost hourly opportunities to spread more fear. What I want to know is how we let ourselves get so dependent on the blinking Russians for all our power. They could have us in darkness at the touch of a button. "

The state opening of parliament caused concern as the Queen was unable to attend, sending her son and grandson as counsellors of state in her place. The Queen's speech, delivered by Prince Charles, included plans for new criminal offences to limit the number of protesters causing disruption by super-gluing themselves to roads.

Finally, in mid-May, a ray of optimism was injected as Sam Ryder's engaging personality and upbeat song got the hostile Eurovision Song Contest audience on side. He won the jury vote with even France giving 12 points, but the public vote saw an unprecedented outpouring of support for the beleaguered Ukraine, giving them the overall win.

After many threats to do so, Isaac finally agreed to stand down as dungeon master and give someone else a go. Jen volunteered, having got furthest with her campaign, based on her all-time favourite movie Labyrinth, featuring David Bowie in a stellar performance amid a bunch of grotesque critters, created by the same stable as the muppets.

# Ch 6 – Start of the Big Adventure

Tangled Warren

    Narrator (Jen) – a Dungeon Master

    Sapphire (Georgie) – a Human teenager

    Avrin (Ben) – the Dwarf king

    Worten (Kev) – a Gnome/goblin halfling

    Bod (Isaac) – a Yeti/ogre cross

    Sir Foxface – Non-Player Character

Nervous in her first role as Dungeon Master, Jen read the script setting the scene, giving the players a chance to get the feel for their chosen characters:

*For nights, Sapphire's dreams were plagued by disturbing images of the impossible Maize Maze and the many puzzles she had to solve. Several years had passed since Avrin, the dwarven king, had kidnapped her baby sister. He'd put every obstacle he could invent in her way to prevent a successful rescue. On the third night, Avrin appeared in his owl-guise, asking for her help.*

*She glared at him. "Why should I help you after everything you subjected me to?"*

*"Because you are a kind and generous person with a thirst for adventure which your mundane life does not provide."*

*She folded her arms as his voice took on a pleading tone. "Please, Sapphire. Hear me out. An evil necromancer has taken over the castle and is turning everything in the labyrinth to the dark side."*

*From what she could remember, most of the*

*enchanted creatures she'd encountered were already pretty warped, but not entirely evil. As she paused, the owl morphed into the king of the dwarves, but nothing like as handsome as in her memories.*

*Tattered clothing hung off his gaunt frame and dark rings encircled his eyes. He sank to the floor in front of her, his arms imploring. "Every day he tortures and maims more of my kind. I understand we didn't treat you very well, but none of them deserves this."*

*Her tender heart was already softening when he dealt the final card. "Yesterday he took one of your dear friends and, knowing him as you do, you can only fear for his life."*

*Sapphire shrank. Who did he mean? Could it be Bod? Or Worten? Images of the gargantuan softy and the truculent scamp flitted through her mind and she raised a quizzical eyebrow.*

*"Sir Foxface." His shrug held sincere apology.*

*Her hand flew to her mouth as she thought of the fierce fighter and his trusty steed. "And Dulux?"*

*"He managed to escape, but he's distraught because he knows his master will fight to the death."*

At Jen's signal, Georgie took over Sapphire's character. "The poor thing."

Ben had picked Avrin's part and, when Jen glanced up, he nodded, adopting Bowie's distinctive flat tones with a surprisingly close impersonation. "Will you help us?"

"Us?" Sapphire narrowed her eyes.

"Me, Worten, Bod and Dulux. If we ever find him. They

are the only creatures the necromancer couldn't bend to his evil will."

"Do I have a choice?"

"Everyone has a choice, but I'm hoping your kind heart and sense of justice will lead you to the right one."

The narrator came in as Sapphire nodded assent.

*Avrin wrapped his arms around her and she clung on as he transformed into an owl and flew to the entrance of a cave. The landing caught her unawares and she stumbled backwards, tumbling into the arms of a huge, white-haired beast with ludicrous eyebrows, who released her, jumping back in fright.*

"Bod, it's me, Sapphire."

He stepped forward, peering at her. "Sapphire friend?"

"Of course, you ninny."

Worten limped up, barely glancing at her. "It's you."

Ignoring his indifference, she hugged him. "I missed you, Worten, even if I don't often dream about you guys."

"'Sno more than I'd expect. Too busy to drop in on your friends, even when they're in dire need."

"I'm sorry. But I'm here now. How can I help?"

He shook his head. "I don't think you can. You may as well go home. There's no point all of us ending up in the stinking swamp, because that's what will happen to anyone who doesn't join the necronamcer."

"You mean necromancer."

"Exactly what I said."

Avrin tutted. "I've given up correcting him. Now you're here we can enlist the help of the good spirits far and wide to lift the enchantment over the city."

"First we must rescue Sir Foxface." Sapphire glared at him.

"I'm afraid that's not possible."

"Why not?" She scented a trap.

Bod howled and Worten wriggled his eyebrows. "Didn't you tell her?"

"Tell me what?" Sapphire glared at the dwarf king, who glanced away. "Has something terrible happened? He can't be …" She broke off with a gulp.

"Dead?" Avrin spat the word. "He's as good as. Stain has him locked away–"

"Stain?"

"The necromancer. He's locked him in the impossible tower."

"Nothing's impossible."

"The mind-boggling puzzles are." Worten folded his arms. "It's also known as the tower of no return."

"Because no one's ever returned from it?"

"I see you've heard of it."

Sapphire rolled her eyes – she'd forgotten his over-developed pedantry. She rounded on Avrin. "Surely you built this tower–"

He held up a hand. "Let me stop you there. My castle had only one tall tower with a winding staircase and four rooms. But there were no traps."

Sapphire brought an image of the castle to mind, but the details were fuzzy. "We need to find out as much as we can. Where's the highest point so we can observe it?"

Worten grumbled. "The cliffs above the stinking swamp. But you mustn't go anywhere near the place – it would be playing straight into his hands."

Bod hopped from one foot to the other. "Owl fly. Seek."

"Of course." Sapphire clapped her hands. "Well done, Bod. It makes perfect sense. Avrin can fly high enough to count the number of towers in the castle." Ignoring the protests forming on the dwarf king's lips, she handed him the dice and he rolled a thirteen.

Warton sniffed. "I don't see why he couldn't fly all the way to the tower and have a good old look at what's going on. That would be much more useful. Just saying."

Before anyone had time to ponder on it, Avrin twirled his cloak which turned into giant wings as he rose upward.

Sapphire noticed how his formerly lush white plumage had dulled to a dirty grey, the feathers sparse and scrappy from undue wear and tear. When she asked the others what had happened to him, Worten shrugged and shuffled off.

Bod shook his head, his chin drooping. "Big battle. Avrin hurt bad. Bod fix."

By dint of careful questioning, considering his inability to answer in more than monosyllables, Sapphire determined the friendly ogre's healing powers.

The narrator took up the tale:

*A massive rumble of thunder drew their attention to the distance where purple clouds broiled. A crack of lightning lit up the castle, revealing two towers. Avrin Magicpalms took up the challenge, flying swift and sure toward the castle, long after his instincts told him it was unsafe to do so. Stung by the sneaky implications of cowardice in his former slave's words, he was determined to do what he could to reset the balance of power in his favour. Concentrating hard, he counted five sets of windows, but before he could get close enough to peek inside, an almighty shriek warned of his detection.*

*Two flying beasts Sapphire would know as pterodactyls attacked from either side, their long beaks pecking his wings and piercing deep into his body.*

*Relying on the hunter's speed and cunning, he dropped as though dead, catching them by surprise as he hurtled to the safety of the forest, hiding in a tree. This was his domain and, as they flew back to the castle, he gingerly crept back to the tunnel entrance, where he collapsed with exhaustion.*

Sapphire glanced at the yeti. "Bod fix Avrin?"

"Too much blood. Avrin die."

The girl trembled, her agitation obvious. "What about if he transformed back to human form?"

"He's not human." Worten scowled. "But he's too weak to transform into anything."

"We can't just let him die. We must do something." Sapphire's gaze implored each of them in turn.

Worten shuffled from one foot to the other. "He would leave one of us if it were the other way around."

"No he wouldn't." Even as she protested, Sapphire knew her words were little more than wishful thinking. "At least … the old Avrin might have done, but he's changed."

Support came from an unexpected quarter as Bod gently picked up the owl's broken body, cradling it in his enormous paws. "Sapphire right. Avrin kind now." A beat, then Isaac's normal voice griped. "Bloody hell, Jen. This thing weighs a ton. Where the hell did you get it from?"

Isaac rarely came out of character – a sure sign he wasn't enjoying this one – and Jen suggested a comfort break. Knowing how he prided himself on his exceptional intellect and planet-sized brain, she'd been surprised when he picked the primitive creature. His insistence had them all picking roles which put them well outside their comfort zone in order to challenge themselves. Because Jen's campaign was much shorter than the others, it seemed the ideal one to try out this experiment.

He persisted with his line of enquiry. "How on earth did you get it up here? Did one of the lads do the heavy lifting? That's not fair, letting them in on it."

"How very dare you?" Jen bristled. "Casting aspersions on my integrity, discretion and physical strength in one fell swoop. Pun intended."

As ever, he failed to spot the tongue placed firmly in her cheek and overcompensated. She let his contrition persist for a couple of sentences before holding up a hand. "I found it in the back shed; I reckon they used it to scare away birds or foxes."

"Birds." Georgie put in. "From the fruit patch. But it wasn't as effective as the twirling CDs. The movement and reflective surface is a much better deterrent."

By this time, Isaac had lost any interest and drifted off to stick the kettle on. Jen addressed the others, using one of her grandad's catch phrases. "What do you think of the show so far?"

"Yeah, it's good." Kev quirked a lip.

"Only good?"

"No, it's great." Georgie jumped in to reassure. "But I'm finding it hard to play the heroine with any degree of credibility. I'm much more of a back-room-boy, me."

"But you can play it however you want. It doesn't have to be anything like in the movie. She's not a 16-year-old would-be drama brat any more. Sarah – sorry, Sapphire – could have become anyone in the intervening years."

"True."

"And she certainly doesn't have to have a huge crush on the dwarf king. Even if he did play out in my head like a yummy cross between Richard Armitage's Thorin Oakenshield and the David Bowie original."

"You can stop putting pictures in my head right now."

Ben grinned. "I thought that was the purpose of a Dungeon Master – to put pictures in our heads."

Kev grimaced. "I must confess to finding this Worten character hard to place. After playing Jinx for so long, in my head he could be his brother."

"Except Worten's not a bard. Charming's the very last thing he is." Ben headed over to the kitchen area.

"True. Maybe I should watch the movie again to get a few pointers."

"Did you not do that already?" Georgie scoffed. "It was the first thing I did after the preparation session. I reckon Ben did too, judging by his perfect accent."

"Did what?" Ben returned with the biscuit tin.

"Watched *Labyrinth*."

"Might have. Are we carrying on? Only I'm gonna need a snack if we're going on much longer."

"I could eat." Kev raised a hand.

"When couldn't you?" Jen squirmed under the pressure of four expectant pairs of eyes and bottled it. Although used to making similar decisions at work, somehow, being solely responsible for other people's enjoyment was a much more onerous task. "How about a show of hands? We could continue for an hour or eat and then decide."

The mood was well and truly broken so, after making a few notes for a smooth resumption, she joined the others in the downstairs kitchen where all hands were preparing dishes for their D&D feast. During the meal, the chat turned to the latest campaign, and Isaac made several anything-but-subtle attempts to get the others to compare Jen's first attempt to the last one.

Ben, ever the diplomat, tried to steer him away. "You can't possibly make a comparison between something a few hours old and the hundreds of hours we spent in the savage caverns."

"Let alone the thousands of hours we've invested in fine-tuning those characters." Kev backed him up. "We have to give it a chance."

Georgie agreed. "I think Jen's started off brilliantly. Just the right amount of action, intrigue and stacks of potential."

"But not a lot of scope for character development, right?"

"That's rubbish. You're just sore because your character doesn't have any flashy magic skills."

"Not at all. I relish the chance to play something large and imposing, but I thought he'd be more of an orc with lots of fighting and battles, not soppy healing."

"Give it a chance, mate." Georgie wagged her finger. "There's nothing soppy about healing."

Jen tried hard not to take it personally. "I did suggest you'd have been better off playing Sir Foxface – he's ferocious."

"But he's only a couple of feet tall and he's not even in the game yet." Isaac's tone took on a familiar wheedling.

"Because whoever was captured by Stain had to be a non-player character." Ben touched her arm. "Take no notice, Jen. He knows full well how it works."

Isaac snorted and Ben addressed him directly. "I think you're mostly struggling with the primitive speech. We can always have Sapphire giving him lessons so he becomes more eloquent."

"But that's cheating." He glared at them. "Isn't it?"

Kev shook his head. "No it's not. You're always telling us it's the players who make the game, so why not?" He reached for the last piece of pork and pickle pie. "These are the best – even yummier than the hard-boiled egg ones."

Isaac pouted. "I wouldn't know, I've not had any."

Kev glanced from the piece of pie mere inches from his mouth to Isaac and back, then caught the eyes of the other three as though requesting help with his quandary. With a deep sigh, he held it out. "You want this last piece?"

After a beat, Isaac sneered. "You think I want it after it's been in your mucky paws? No thank you."

"What nonsense. I touched it with my extremely clean hands when I cut it up."

"In that case …" Isaac made a grab for it, but Kev saw the play coming a mile off and snatched his hand away, biting it in half. "Mmm. So much more than yummy – it's ambrosia."

Jen and Georgie shared a matching eye-roll – the way Isaac fell for Kev's teasing every time never failed to amuse. More often than not it was well deserved after Isaac had taken yet another opportunity to patronise, denigrate or belittle. For whatever reason, he never did it to Ben – or at the very least, it was far less toxic.

At the end of the meal, as Kev opened the third bottle of wine, Ben sought everyone's opinion about playing on, but the consensus was a re-run of the movie.

As Jen tried hard not to equate this with abject failure to engage them, he whispered a soft encouragement.

"Don't take it to heart. I think we'll all benefit from a re-assessment of the source material now we're playing the game in earnest. Until then it was all a tad ephemeral."

She giggled. "Or even ethereal. As in insubstantial rather than fleeting."

He brazened out the blush reddening all the way to the tips of his ears. "That too. And after almost half a bottle of wine, certain individuals will be in need of a restorative sleep before continuing."

She followed his gaze to where Isaac's eyelids were definitely drooping, and clinked her glass with his. "I'll drink to that."

# Ch 7 – The New Big Bad

Tangled Warren
    Jack of Diamonds/Spades – Non player characters
    Hermit – Non player character
    Flameys – Non player characters


Saturday saw an early start to the gaming as they all felt inspired after watching the actions of the characters on whom theirs were based.

Jen delighted in their progress as they navigated through her version of the labyrinth to reach the four guards, who she'd re-imagined as playing cards, namely the jacks of diamonds and spades.

The Jack of Diamonds challenged them. "You can only ask your question if you know which of the kings has no moustache."

"Have a heart. How are we possibly supposed to know without a deck of cards?" Worten grumbled.

"Is that your answer?" The playing card demanded.

"Why bother asking?" The Jack of Spades sneered. "You know we have to take the first thing they say. So yes, it *is* the King of Hearts."

"You knave. You're always spoiling my fun." The Jack of Diamonds sulked. "Go on then. Ask your question."

"Wait a moment." Sapphire narrowed her eyes. "If you have to take the first thing we say, we must confer before asking anything."

"That's not in the rules." The Jack of Spades glared.

"Just because it isn't in the rules doesn't mean we can't do it." Sapphire beckoned the others out of earshot as the four heads argued vociferously about the regulations.

She charged her fellows that, because they were only allowed one question, they mustn't waste it on something daft like "what are the rules?"

Ben groaned. "It's like the game at school when you're not allowed to say yes or no. I was never any good at it."

He'd obviously forgotten he was supposed to be at death's door and unable to speak, but nobody noticed so Jen let it go, thrilled by how they were all so caught up in her trickery.

Sapphire scanned around. "What about the rest of you?"

"No good asking me anything to do with puzzles." Worten sniffed. "I'm rubbish at them."

Bod growled in frustration. "Bod know puzzles."

Worten scoffed. "Yes, but you can't speak well enough to ask the right question. It must be you."

Sapphire winced. "I can't believe it. Last night, Sarah made solving the puzzle seem so easy, but now I can't think straight."

Worten glared at her. "You're a bag of nerves. It's affecting your ability to think straight. Calm down."

Flinching at the harsh truth, she nodded. "All right. Only I will speak. If you have an answer, write it in the dirt. Okay?"

They nodded and she approached the cards. "First you must explain the rules."

"You're only allowed one question." The Jack of Diamonds folded his arms triumphantly.

"I didn't ask a question."

"Didn't she?" The Jack of Diamonds tilted his head.

The Jack of Spades rolled his eyes. "No, it was a statement; her voice didn't go up at the end. I'll do it. One of these doors leads to the enchanted grove, and the other to certain death. Apart from the one question thing, one of us always tells the truth and the other always lies."

"Got it." As she hesitated, Bod leapt up and down, pointing to the ground where he'd drawn a picture.

It seemed to confirm her memory and she approached the grumpy Jack of Spades, speaking with some confidence. "If I ask the Jack of Diamonds if his door leads to the enchanted grove, would he say yes?"

The card thought about it for a moment, and then said, a little uncertainly, "No?"

"Then that's the right door. Come on, guys."

Bod whooped with delight, capering after her, carrying the owl. They passed through cautiously, expecting a nefarious trap, but none appeared, and the ground didn't open up into a bottomless pit full of helping hands.

Worten grumbled. "I still don't get it."

Sapphire reduced it to the headlines. "The Jack of Spades told the truth, that the Jack of Diamonds would lie and say his was the wrong door."

"But what if Spades lied?"

"Then Diamonds would have said "Yes," because he told the truth, but Spades would lie and say "No.""

Worten's frown deepened. "But what if Diamonds was standing in front of the door to sudden death?"

She thought for a moment. "The answer would have been 'Yes' whoever was lying."

"Aarrgghh." He clutched his head. "Brain ache. La-la-

la-la, la-la-la-la." As he stamped his feet in time to the notes, a beautiful butterfly landed on Bod's finger.

"What a pretty butterfly." Worten held out his hand and the insect flitted onto his finger. "Ouch."

"What happened?" Sapphire spun around.

"It bit me."

Bod shook his head. "Butterfly bad. So sad." He swiped at it clumsily and it flew away.

With a sigh, Sapphire kissed Worten's hand better. "Come on. The sooner we get to the Enchanted Glade, the better."

Unfortunately, the once-magical place was overgrown with thick briars, and the narrator warned them not to disturb them. "They will screech at the slightest touch and alert the necromancer to the presence of adventurers seeking good magic."

Worten rolled a fifteen which allowed him to traverse the hazardous path to reach the healing well and draw up a pail of murky, stagnant water.

"Try again." Sapphire's tone encouraged, but the second one showed scant improvement and the narrator reminded he only had three chances.

"Wait. Try putting a stone in the bottom of the pail to force it deeper, below the surface."

Despite shaking his head, Worten followed her suggestion and the third attempt resulted in much purer water, although it lacked the normal sparkling clarity.

Bod rolled eighteen and, with his proficiency bonus, gained enough healing power to restore the dwarven king sufficient to take a turn. But having lost so many hit points on the attack, he had to stay as an owl for two more turns to recover enough to transform back and regain his powers.

The others used their turns to forage for supplies, and Sapphire took the opportunity to teach Bod new words to expand his limited vocabulary, along with a few rules about sentence construction.

When Avrin finally returned to humanoid form, Sapphire noted how much his appearance had improved – not to his former glory, but he no longer looked at death's door.

He bowed deeply. "Thank you, my friends. I am forever in your debt for agreeing to help. However, I haven't been entirely honest with you."

"I knew it." Worten grimaced. "Never trust a king whose main form of amusement is torture."

"Ouch. The truth always hurts. Dear Wortle, I apologise for the many torments you have endured at my behest."

"It's Worten, not Wortle." He shifted from foot to foot.

"Sorry. You're right again. I must make more effort to call you by your right name. Names are so important and it's a lack of respect to keep mangling yours."

"Do get on with it." Bod folded his long arms. "What haven't you told us?"

"Oh, dear. It seems the ability to speak better has changed your sunny nature. But no matter. In order to restore the creatures, we must travel throughout the kingdom collecting certain items which will enhance the magical energy from all the good spirits."

Sapphire saw the reluctance from the other two and

wanted to focus on the quest instead of indulging their squabbles. "What are these items and where will we find them?"

"A good question." His gaze went inward, but the effort of trying to retrieve the information taxed him. "I did know, but my memories have not been completely restored. I do remember they have to be collected in a particular order ..." He tried again, resulting in a pained wince, but his dice roll wasn't sufficient to supply the details.

The narrator took pity on Avrin's fragile state. "All is not lost as the dwarven king remembers he obtained the list from an ancient oak in the Wild Wood."

Sapphire sighed. "I suppose we're going there next. I wish I had a map of this place so I could determine the best path." She rolled, but her score didn't allow access to the map. The narrator supplied a few details and she scribbled a rough plan.

"You are at the northernmost part of the kingdom, and the Wicked Wastelands stretch as far as the eye can see to the west and for a mile to the south where they meet the Junkyard. This runs from the eastern border of the Enchanted Glade until it meets the Crumbling Cliffs which provide the eastern boundary.

"Which direction is the Wild Wood?"

"South east of here, but if you go as the crow flies, you will encounter the Stinking Swamp."

"Which runs all the way from the junkyard to the river." Avrin pointed to the shape on her sketch and she labelled it, along with several pertinent features.

"Wait. The hermit's cave is at the foot of the cliffs, and

he will lead us across them to the woods." Worten adjusted his cap, obviously pleased with himself.

"For a price." Bod added.

Enchanted Glade

Hermit's Cave

Healing Well

Wicked Wasteland

Junk Yard

Crumbling Cliffs

Monstrous Mountains

Stinking

Castle

Fearsome Forest

Swamp

Dwarf City

Ravaging River

Wild Wood

"First we have to cross the junkyard, and if the junk lady is under Stain's control–"

"Bod will disarm her." Worten's mouth twisted as he interrupted Avrin. "She has a soft spot for him."

"Junk lady like Bod. A lot." He nodded agreement, his eyebrows wriggling as he rolled the dice. The twelve was just enough for him to distract her while the others snuck past. Reverting back to primitive speech patterns proved a great benefit, allowing him to play dumb when she fired questions at him.

At the cave, Worten used his turn to summon the hermit, but he wouldn't even appear until they told him which of the four kings didn't hold a sword.

Sapphire closed her eyes. "Definitely one of the red suits, but which one?"

"I'll have to hurry you."

She huffed a sigh of relief as the picture in her mind sharpened. "Diamonds. He carries an axe."

The narrator displayed a picture of the four kings, but when the boys tried to study them, she snatched it away to cries of, "That's not fair."

"You say that phrase so often – I wonder about your basis for comparison."

Avrin caught the narrator's reference to the goblin king's quote in the movie and grinned. "I think we're seeing evidence of a youth misspent playing poker."

The narrator scoffed. "It was patience, actually. But after the question came up in a quiz, I studied all the royal cards looking for odd-one-outs."

On the hermit's turn, he demanded payment for guiding them through the cliff-top path, exaggerating the dangers. "The way is treacherous and a wrong step could have you tumbling over the edge into the putrid swamp below."

Worten offered three of the many bangles he carried.

The hermit scoffed. "They're rubbish. Show me your most precious one."

Hesitating, Worten snuck an arm behind his back, but

the wizened old man saw it and wrenched his arm forward cruelly as he inspected the gaudy bracelet.

"Huh, it's merely plastic beads – totally worthless."

"But Sapphire gave it to me."

A derisive snort. "You're even more stupid than I took you for. What else?" Dismissing Bod's stone, he peered at Sapphire's hairclip and necklace, but his greedy gaze was caught by Avrin rolling one of his charmed crystals between his fingers. The others looked alarmed, but the dwarf king assured them he had two more left and they agreed it was worth the risk.

With payment agreed, the wizened creature led them up a hidden path to the top of the cliffs where, although they were many hundreds of feet above the swamp, they caught the odd whiff of the noxious fumes. He made a big deal of stamping his staff on the ground, occasionally causing a minor avalanche and muttering about "One wrong step."

Sapphire rejoiced when they reached the end of the path, but their next problem involved scrambling down to the woods below.

The hermit rubbed his hands together, adopting a casual tone. "You could attempt it on your own, but one–"

"Wrong step." They chorused the refrain.

"I *could* show you, but it will cost another crystal."

Sapphire refused politely, thanking for his service, and he went off, grumbling they'd never find the way without him.

Bod griped. "I hope you know what you're doing."

She winked, muttering, "Trust me." Then, louder, "I think we should stop for some lunch before continuing."

Something about the man felt off, and she waited until he was well out of earshot before explaining about the series of steps she'd spotted cut into the rock. They led to a path beside the waterfall, and they took it in turns to see how much damage they would incur getting to the bottom.

Only Bod suffered a hit point, but he had more than the rest, so it all balanced out. Leaving him to recover, they each scouted a little way down the three paths leading from the waterfall, but when they returned he was nowhere to be seen. A mournful howl led them to a clearing where he hung, upside-down, suspended by ropes around his feet. Several furry orange creatures had built a fire underneath him and capered around, dancing and joking.

Avrin pulled the other two behind a bush. "Flameys."

"Oh, no. I remember these things." Sapphire groaned. "They were evil before, so goodness knows how dreadful they'll be now. Totally obsessed with removing heads."

"My fault, I'm afraid." Avrin gave a small, apologetic shrug. "I was experimenting with goblins and fire demons and they were the result. But they were never meant to be evil, just fun-loving scamps."

"Having my limbs pulled off is not my idea of fun."

He nudged her shoulder. "Honestly, they're armless." Avrin's coy glance invited her to share his endearing chuckle, and she couldn't help herself.

Another howl reminded them of Bod's predicament and Worten hissed at the dwarf king. "You should do something; after all, it's your fault."

His eyes narrowed as he watched them poking and prodding the huge, hairy lump. "The trouble is, if they are under the necromancer's spell, he'll know where to find me the second they see me."

"Coward."

"No, Worten, he's not being cowardly." Sapphire jumped in to defend. "It makes sense for Avrin not to reveal himself since they all know him."

Before he could protest further, she stepped into the clearing. "Let him go by order of your ruler."

"Hey, Lady. No one rules us, we's free spirits."

"True and true." The others agreed.

"If you want to remain free, you must let him go. Now."

"Oh. Why didn't you say so?" The one who seemed to be the leader doffed his royal blue cap.

"I just did." She recoiled as they released the beast so rapidly he fell to the ground. "So you don't serve Stain?"

"The necromancer? Never." His head swivelled a full turn while the blue cap remained stationary.

"He sucks all the joy out of life." A second one scrunched huge black eyebrows.

"What about Avrin?" Sapphire put her hands on her hips.

"What about him?" Blue-cap winked.

"You tell me."

"Tell you what?"

"About Avrin." Huffing a sigh, she realised his quick-fire teasing was designed to enrage and made her question more specific. "Is Avrin evil too?"

"Only when he has to be. Most of the time he's just mischievous. Like us."

"I'm nothing like you." Avrin pushed into the clearing

and the orange creatures capered around him, climbing on his back and clinging to his limbs until he could no longer walk. With a grunt, he shook himself and they fell to the ground in a heap of disconnected body parts, which hopped around, reassembling themselves into the five zany critters.

"We heard you was dead." Blue-cap poked a bony finger in the king's chest.

"Rumours of my demise were greatly exaggerated. So you haven't joined Stain's campaign to spread fear and hatred throughout the land?"

"How could you even ask?" The one with black eyebrows folded his arms which promptly came out of their shoulder sockets and fell to the floor.

One of the others picked up the bony arms, using them as drumsticks on the ribs of a third.

Blue-cap rolled his eyes all the way back into their sockets. "We keeps ourselves to ourselves. Don't follow no ruler's plans."

"Don't I know it." Avrin scoffed. "So you'll help us destroy him?"

Worten came out of hiding. "Us? Who's us?"

The leader shrieked. "Worten never helps anyone but himself."

"Except when the whole kingdom's in danger." Avrin wagged a finger. "Then it's the duty of every right-minded citizen to do their bit."

Black eyebrows' head swivelled all the way around. "Don't mean us then. Not one of us is in their right mind." He kicked the drummer, who restored his arms, putting them on the wrong way around, then ran away, giggling.

With a growl, the flamey turned his head and lower body to suit. "Nor never will be."

"Come on. This lot are wasting our time." Bod forgot to use mono-syllables.

Blue-cap picked up on it straight away. "Bod speaks proper now. There's posh."

Black eyebrows went further. "Bod's no fun anymore. Worten's turned soft and Avrin's king of nothing. All because of a silly girl who doesn't play fair."

Sapphire cringed. She'd hoped they'd forgotten the previous visit when her character threw all their heads away in her bid to escape.

"I remember her." The drummer leered. "You owe us a head, Lady."

Despite the terror of the memory, she stood her ground. "No I don't."

"You broke the rules. You're only allowed to throw your own head." Others joined in the chant.

"That's not true. *He* threw *his* head first." She pointed at two of them and, as predicted, it started a vociferous argument between them about the rules and they started chucking each other's heads around.

Avrin signalled for the gang to sneak away, but they hadn't got far when the critters came bounding up, demanding satisfaction.

The dwarf king glared sternly. "You mongrels will never be satisfied. It's in your nature to always want more. I say the only way you will get real fulfilment is by doing something generous and useful which will benefit others."

"Sounds too much like hard work." Blue-cap pouted.

"But it would be so much fun." Avrin's tone cajoled.

"Sound's cool. What would we have to do?"

"Very little. Just confuse, confound and delay anyone who comes here looking for us."

"But that's exactly what we already do."

"Then do it more. Pretend you know where we're going and lead them into the Stinking Swamp."

Black eyebrows clapped his hands. "It does sound like fun. Especially the bit when they're writhing around screaming about the stench."

"Then we have a deal?"

"Deal!" They all spat on their palms and shook hands.

"Now go and find your first victims."

When they'd gone, Worten groused. "I think you're a fool to trust them."

Avrin's hand shot out to encircle the grumpy gnome's squat neck. "Nobody calls me a fool and gets away with it."

Worten choked out an apology. "S-s-sorry, your lordship. I didn't mean anything by it."

"No, Wortle, you never do. I've had enough of your insubordination." He squeezed until the gnome's features turned purple.

"Stop it, Avrin, you'll kill him." Sapphire tugged at his arm, but he shook her off easily with a twisted smile.

"That's the idea."

# Ch 8 – Platinum Jubilee

June 2022 – Season 4

June brought with it a huge boost as the year-long activities surrounding the Queen's Platinum Jubilee took over, giving the whole country cause for celebration. Every TV channel devoted prime-time hours to coverage of the events and the whole country festooned itself in red, white and blue. Local councils had obviously planned for months as bright displays welcomed visitors to villages, towns and cities all over the country.

Georgie was given the task of overseeing the many floral tributes in the centre of town and she spent hours researching previous years' displays and coordinating with nearby towns to present a cohesive theme. The jubilee coincided with hosting the Commonwealth Games in Birmingham so every roundabout of the ring-road encircling the town featured emblems from the larger countries, such as Canada and Australia, surrounded by flags from many more.

On Thursday 2nd June, Isaac surprised them all at dinner by suggesting they watched the highlights of the first day of what he called "Lilibet's birthday bash."

Kev paused in the act of helping himself to a second portion of mash. "Since when did you become a royalist?"

"I'm not. But my family were, and you can't help but admire the woman for still being active after seventy years. She's ninety-six, for goodness sake."

His vehemence caused an awkward silence which Georgie filled. "I'd love to. Gran loved the Queen, and I must say I'd like the opportunity to share in her celebrations, after all we did get an extra bank holiday."

"That's tomorrow. Today is for Whitsun – they always move it to the Monday closest to the end of May." Kev speared the last sausage.

"Okay, Mr Pedant. No one's forcing you to watch it if you don't want to."

"Nah, I'll check it out. Wouldn't want to watch the whole thing, but a few highlights are cool."

Isaac's motivation for wanting them all to watch soon became clear as he took the commentators to task each time they didn't explain something to his satisfaction. "No, it actually *is* her seventieth trooping of the colour."

Jen had to call him on it. "Not if it was cancelled in 1955 because of the rail strike as he said."

Isaac sniffed. "But she actually took the salute in the year before her coronation because the king was ill."

Jen hissed. "Shhh – I'm missing this. Something about when she stopped riding on horseback."

"That would be 1986 when she rode Burmese for the last time and started using a carriage."

"I heard *that*, but why?"

"Because she was too old?" Ben ventured. "She'd have been in her sixties."

"Rubbish. Princess Anne's still doing it at seventy."

"Maybe she was put off because of the guy who shot at her." Ben gestured at the screen, but none of the others had heard the throwaway comment.

"You're kidding, right? When was it?" They focussed on the screen, hoping for more details, but it was time for the final royal salute and the commentary moved swiftly on to show the 41-gun salute.

Isaac found it first. "1981. A disgruntled teenager inspired by the assassination of John Lennon and the attempts on the US President and the Pope. But he only fired blanks and she managed to calm her horse."

Ben glowered. "I hope they locked him up and threw away the key."

"Nope. He got five years for treason, but they let him out after three, and he sent her an apology letter."

Next came the flypast of over seventy aircraft, which included typhoon jets forming the number 70, the Battle of Britain memorial flight and several helicopters which had seen service in Ukraine. As always, the Red Arrows ended the show with their red, white and blue smoke trails.

The program section ended, to be replaced by live coverage from several of the Queen's homes where people waited for the signal to light various beacons, varying from huge bonfires to slender, gas-fuelled beacons. The report showed a range of the braziers of all shapes and sizes as communities up and down the country joined in, hosting medieval-style parties with mead and roast chestnuts.

"Three and a half thousand – that's a heck of a lot of towns and villages – how many are there in the UK?"

"Over forty thousand." Isaac loved the chance to show off his encyclopaedic knowledge of trivia. "But the figure you quoted is from all over the world, not just here."

"You mean the commonwealth."

"Exactly."

As Isaac agreed, the commentator drew their attention

to the fragile figure in her turquoise-blue coat and trademark pearls waiting in the quadrangle of Windsor Castle while the chief yeoman placed the vivid blue sphere on the stand. Her white-gloved-hand stretched out to press the globe which triggered the lighting of the first beacon. Over in Buckingham Palace, her grandson, William watched with others as the "Tree of trees" lit up.

Georgie perked up at the mention of the 70ft sculpture. "I read about this, it's very clever. It's one foot for each year of her reign, and there are 350 native British trees–"

"Five for every year." Isaac snuck in.

She ignored the interruption. "In pots made from reclaimed materials, reflecting the royal family's concern for the environment."

"And the whole thing looks like a giant tree." Jen grinned. "Awesome."

They watched the footage of fires being lit all over the world, followed by the forty-three  beacons of the Royal Institute of Chartered Surveyors' anchor chain which extended throughout the four nations of the UK. At nine forty-five, the rest of the UK lit up, and the spectacle ended at ten when archers lit the beacons along Hadrian 's Wall.


The following day started bright and clear, with the promise of a warm day and, like many people, they drove to the coast. Walking along the beach helped work up an appetite for the traditional fish and chips on the pier. They rather unwisely followed this with some of the fun fair rides until Kev nearly chucked up, at which point they found a pub with a garden. On the way back, they planned a party for the following evening while they watched the much-publicised Platinum Party at the Palace.

"You do realise everyone else will be doing their big jubilee lunch on the Sunday." Isaac turned around to address Jen and Georgie, who sat either side of Kev in Ben's Fiesta. He insisted on sitting in the front because he reckoned the back of the car gave him motion-sickness.

"And we should care because …?" Kev glared at him.

"I'm just saying."

Jen sensed the tension between them, putting it down to the discomfort of the hard middle seat. Kev's gallantry in "taking one for the team" gave him an excuse to spread his legs either side of the transmission tunnel, making it hard for the girls to avoid thigh-to-thigh contact, no matter how much they squeezed to the edge of the seat.

Ben piped up from the front. "No reason we can't do both – there's always plenty left over from a party, so we can just save some stuff to cook the next day."

"Sounds like a plan. I wonder if her maj will make it to the party tonight." Georgie looked up from her phone. "I just read she missed the Service of Thanksgiving at St Paul's Cathedral today because she 'experienced some discomfort' during the flypast."

"It's got to be a bit much for someone in her nineties. Imagine having to do all that smiling and waving when you're in pain." Jen suffered from awful monthly cramps.

"It would be hard for anyone at any age. It says here she had to watch the Epsom Derby on TV and you know how much she loves horse-racing."

"Maybe *you* know. I never realised you were such a

Queen-o-phile. Are we dressing up tomorrow? Does it have to be red, white and blue?" Isaac pouted.

Georgie had opened her mouth at his initial remark, but the protest – if that's what she intended – stayed put as she answered his last question. "We could each pick a decade from her reign. Or a commonwealth country."

"I bagsy Australia. I'll stick some corks around my hat."

"Now you've given it away. The idea is the rest of us have to guess." Kev rolled his eyes.

Ben caught his gaze in the rear-view mirror. "We could do one or the other – or even both."

"It'll be tricky with no time to prepare." Jen glanced at Isaac. "Unless we use the clothes in the time capsule."

He sniffed. "I suppose we could. But we'd have to use the overalls. And wash the stuff afterwards."

In the end, only three of them used the clothes in the capsule. Jen had a white tee shirt with a red maple leaf, teaming it with a shiny blue rock-and-roll skirt and vintage bolero cardigan. Short white socks and a tartan bow in her hair completed the 50s Canada theme. Georgie went for a classic black-and-white Mary Quant mini-dress, teamed with knee-high white boots and Ben went full-on 70s hippie. A psychedelic tie-die shirt with fringed brown-suede waistcoat sat atop the widest bell-bottomed jeans Jen had ever seen. The bright, crocheted Rasta cap complete with dreadlocks confirmed the country as Jamaica.

But Kev stole the show with a pair of dark corduroy trousers cut-off below the knee, a matching waistcoat and huge hairy feet. He wore a blue flag as a cloak with the union jack in the corner and four stars.

"I thought Isaac was doing Australia." Ben winked at the others as Isaac walked in dressed as a poor man's Crocodile Dundee in leather and khaki.

"Different flag mate." Kev displayed the Northern Cross. "My stars are red in the middle, there's only four of them and they're pentagrams. The Aussie flag has six white stars and most of them are heptagrams."

"You mean seven-sided, right?" Jen narrowed her eyes. "So it's New Zealand, but what decade?"

Isaac glanced at the outfit and scowled. "Can't be the thirties when the Hobbit was written, because it was before she came to power. Lord of the Rings was mid-fifties."

"But Jen's doing the fifties." Kev gestured at her outfit with a flourish. "And anyway, I was thinking of a more recent decade."

"It must be the noughties." Ben grinned.

"Because?"

"It's more Frodo than Bilbo – he never wore a cloak."

"Is that it?" Kev raised a quizzical brow.

"And the *Hobbit* movies were all released between 2012 and 2014, but *Lord of the Rings* were early noughties."

"Bingo!" Kev held up a palm and Ben high-fived. "So we have 50s, 60s and 70s – I guess yours must be 80s."

Isaac echoed Kev's earlier tone. "Because?"

"It's when the Crocodile Dundee movies were made."

"But I look nothing like him."

"Truer words were never spoken."

The girls exchanged eye rolls, dragging them into the lounge where they'd put a trestle table facing the massive OLED TV. They heaped their plates amid the usual banter and Georgie had to shush them when the show started.

As the camera followed a footman walking through the palace, Isaac scoffed. "Are you on the right channel? This looks like one of the mockumentaries they seem to be running on every channel this weekend." He stared as a furry face filled the screen. "Wait, what?"

"It's Paddington Bear." Kev chuckled as the white-haired regent proposed, "Tea" with a raised eyebrow.

"That's not really her." Isaac peered at the screen.

Ben shrugged. "I might have agreed until she did the thing with Daniel Craig for the Olympics."

They all watched in delight as the scene played out with the Queen showing a variety of facial expressions at the clumsy bear's antics, even delivering a few lines about where she kept her marmalade sandwich.

Jen felt her eyes watering – there was something so precious about this powerful woman who refused to take herself so seriously she couldn't enjoy a few moments of cheeky, heart-warming joy.

It ended with the pair of them tapping their teacups in time to Queen's *We Will Rock You* and Georgie broke into spontaneous applause. "I've seen a couple of things where people say she has a real naughty side – she certainly seemed to enjoy it."

Ben nodded. "And she's quite the actress – it would all have been green screened."

"Surely someone's pretending to be Paddington."

"Of course, otherwise the eye-line wouldn't be right. But it's not the same as watching the animated version."

"And you know this because …?"

"I spent some time in the studio last year. It was cool."

"Like the making-of videos on the Hobbit with Andy Serkis?" Kev winked.

The concert opened with Queen doing three of their best with Adam Lambert filling in for Freddie, and continued with a mix of golden oldies, modern and musicals. It had something for everyone, including Sam Ryder's almost-Eurovision-winning *Spaceman* and Andrea Bocelli's *Nessun Dorma*.

They struggled to pick a stand-out performance, but all agreed the production team deserved a mention for the phenomenal special effects like a river of fire cascading down from Buckingham Palace – which became the largest backdrop for fabulous wildlife films. Meanwhile, the royal ballet school performed on a stage around the tree of trees, accompanied by a personal message expressing how proud the Queen was of the men in her life, followed by a poignant reply from Prince William.

This section touched Georgie, who openly sobbed all the way through, missing the end of Celeste's rendition of *Wonderful World*. Ben paused the TV to give her time to sluice her face and compose herself, and he opened a bottle of prosecco so they could share a toast on her return.

Stephen Fry's humble introduction set them up for more heart-string tugging as the future king delivered a touching speech to "Mummy." When the national anthem began, they stood and raised their glasses. After a swig, Georgie began singing and the others joined in, starting a little self-consciously, but getting into the swing of it, even waving the union jacks along with the thousands in the crowd.

"Thank goodness they didn't do the second verse – I've no idea how it goes." Kev was first to drop his flag and sit.

"Something about scattering her enemies and frustrating their knavish tricks." Ben surprised them all, taking on a defensive tone. "What? We learnt it in junior school."

Before Isaac could recite it in full, their attention was drawn to the image of a bone floating above the castle where a huge, grinning corgi awaited.

"What the what?" Kev voiced their thoughts.

"It's all done with drones." Isaac's tone belittled.

"There must be dozens." Georgie stared at the Queen's trademark handbag opening to release several red hearts.

"Several hundred, I'd imagine." He peered closer.

The cameras focussed on the singer and dancers, causing protests as the lads wanted to see more of the drone show – this technology was dear to their hearts.

At the end of the concert, Kev suggested they'd have been better off recording the show and watching with a time delay so they could fast forward past the boring bits.

"Funny you should say that, because I've already set it up to record the pageant tomorrow." Georgie grinned.

"Oh, God. Don't tell me there's more. I thought they ended with the party."

"Doesn't she deserve a big fuss after seventy years?"

"It's not that, I ..." Kev quirked a lip. "Sorry. I meant no disrespect, it's just my memories of long parades aren't the best. Don't get me wrong, I loved the Disney ones in Paris, but I hated standing in the rain to watch my cousins."

"No one's forcing you to watch it if you have something better to do." She folded her arms.

"I'd prefer to move on with Jen's campaign, I'm enjoying it far more than I expected to and we left it with Avrin trying to strangle poor Worten."

"No reason we can't do both." Ben clapped him on the back. "Remind me what time it's on."

Georgie checked her phone. "Two thirty till five."

"We've got rugger training in the morning, but we could maybe have the meal around four and watch a few highlights. Then we can play afterwards."

"Meaning you want us to have the food ready for when you get back?" Jen glared at them.

"Not at all. There's a stack of left-overs, and we can sort out the extra food if you guys want to watch the early bits. Assuming you like all the pipes and drums stuff."

"What? How do you know it'll start with that?"

"It's on the net: starts with a military parade, and ends with Ed Sheeran singing – no doubt *Perfect*."

"What a treat for us all. Really not selling this." Kev grimaced, ducking as Georgie threw a cushion at him.

Having another party meal minimised the clearing up after Saturday and meant no set-up on Sunday.

While the boys were out, the girls did their bit towards the meal, then Jen went upstairs to work on the next D&D session, leaving Georgie on the sofa with a glass of wine, re-watching her favourite bits of the central weekend. When the pageant started, Ben was right, the first half hour showed various armed forces from across the commonwealth, each sporting their colours proudly, stiffening up as they passed by the platform where the next two future kings of England sat with their wives. The

107

military spectacle had a cast of a least two thousand people and a few hundred horses.

She was glad of the opportunity to watch it on her own – her granddad had been in the army and he'd always loved the regimental music – even the bagpipes. Watching the precision drills, she imagined his comments as he'd point out any arm a few inches out, or a leg not in perfect unison. It brought him back in the room with her, and she appreciated the solitude as tears once again flowed.

The next half hour started with Queen's *Bicycle Race* and three hundred cyclists, led by several Olympic medallists. She'd missed the introduction and zoomed back to discover it was the "Time of our Lives" section portraying seventy years of British life. Each decade had its own music, fashions, dance styles and cars, accompanied by open-top double-decker buses wrapped in custom-made graphics depicting each decade's major events. Several national treasures from all walks of life were packed into each bus, waving at the crowd and singing along. Various floats and other vehicles depicted icons of each period, from space hoppers to diggers, Northern Soul to Disco.

The progress of the parade was slow with several gaps, and far too much time devoted to picking out famous faces and the reactions of the royals in their custom-built shelter. When the boys turned up, Kev watched a bit and announced he'd probably just catch the highlights on the news, then went to help Ben in the kitchen.

Georgie only needed to watch a few minutes of the next section, "Let's Celebrate," to know this was much more like it, so she wound the recording back to the purpleshirted flash mob and noted the time-stamp. The yummy smells filling the air suggested the food was well on the way and she followed her nose to discover Jen directing the lads in a piece of choreography worthy of any of the previous night's acts.

"Typical." Isaac scoffed. "You turn up when there's nothing left to do."

"Pots and kettles – you only got here a minute ago."

Jen and Ben swapped eye rolls at Kev's accusation – he was easily the second worst in the skiving stakes. Shaking her head, Georgie fetched the hostess trolley out of what Isaac called the pantry and loaded it with hot dishes.

With five of them on the task, they quickly transferred the food to the lounge and, as they crammed their plates with a little bit of everything, Georgie found the right spot and started playing. As she'd predicted, it didn't take long for them to be pretty much glued to the screen – even Kev. Each troupe brought their own ideas as thousands of people contributed their time, effort and skills to showing exactly what was great about this country. The commentary came into its own, describing the creativity of each of the main regions involved and explaining how each display related to the Queen's extraordinary life experience.

By skipping through everyone's least favourite bits, they caught up to real time at the point where the Queen came out on the balcony in a bright green coat, surrounded by a greatly reduced entourage. Afterwards, they left everything covered in a tablecloth as they resumed the campaign from its cliff-hanger ending.

# Ch 9 – The Ancient Oak

Tangled Warren

Sapphire desperately wanted to believe Avrin wasn't evil, but the cruel sneer warping his features said otherwise. Glaring at him, she summoned all her strength and courage to wrench his arm hard enough to loosen his grip and Bod pulled Worten out of his vicious grasp.

Avrin stumbled back with a confused blink, gesturing at his former victim. "What the heck? Sorry, Worten. I can't apologise enough. I have no idea what came over me."

A screech overhead had them scanning the skies and Bod's keen eyesight picked out the two pterodactyls way above them. He pointed. "Bad birds. Hide."

They didn't need telling twice as each made a dash for the plentiful cover. As before, the flying reptiles' massive wingspan meant they couldn't follow into the woods and they had to return to the castle without completing their mission. *Or did they?*

Something bothered Sapphire. "How did they know where to find us?"

Avrin narrowed his eyes. "Stain has spies everywhere."

"But we haven't seen anyone except the flameys."

"And the hermit." Worten continued to rub his throat.

"I didn't trust him when he demanded another crystal." Bod shook his head.

"You should have seen his face when you refused him." Worten glanced at the dwarf king. "His expression was right cunning."

"Which you would know all about." Bod sneered.

"Stop picking on Worten, you two."

The gnome preened at Sapphire's words, but then she turned on him. "And as for you – why didn't you say something earlier? We need to know who we can trust."

"That's easy. Nobody." Avrin's face soured. "Not even yourself."

Sapphire's head jerked up. "What do you mean?"

"Those terry things – as you call them – controlled my mind, forcing me to try and hurt Worten. I would never do such a thing normally."

"Really?" Bod's expression said otherwise.

"It's true." Worten nodded. "He's done many rotten things, but he's never tried to cause physical pain."

"Yet he's happy for his minions to inflict all manner of horrors." Bod shuddered, his long hair rippling around him.

"I wouldn't say happy–"

"Enough." Sapphire felt cracks in their tenuous bonds, already weakened by the horrible energies in the place. "Forget what happened in the past. Right now we need to trust each other or this won't work."

The others exchanged wary glances and she tutted. "We should all keep an eye on the others and if we see someone acting out of character, bring them to their happy place."

"Where's that?"

"I don't know. It will be different for each of us. Mine is my eleventh birthday – the last time I saw my real mum."

As the others recalled their best time, Sapphire was touched when both Worten and Avrin mentioned meeting her. Bod's face, however, puckered up as he refused to say.

"Stop being such a prat." Worten slapped his arm. "We

all know it was the same for you. None of our lives had any meaning till she came along."

"Whatever." Bod sniffed. "Instead of wasting time on cute memories, we should be heading to this old tree."

"Never call him that. The Ancient Oak has ruled these lands for longer than any other king, and if he senses a lack of respect, you'll never find your way out of the Wild Wood."

Bod snorted, but Avrin's fierce glare shut him up.

Sapphire sensed something more. "Is there anything else we should know about this special oak? He sounds powerful."

"He's certainly that. Take care of your thoughts around him, try to be positive and generous. It won't be a problem for you, but ..." He glared meaningfully behind her.

"He can read minds?"

"Not quite, but very close. Every thought has a distinctive energy and he senses it."

She glanced at the other two and Avrin picked up on her concern, clapping them on the back. "While Sapphire and I meet with the king of the forest, I have an extremely important job for you both. Worten, you should hide in these bushes and keep watch for any of Stain's followers approaching from the north or east."

"Do I have to fight them?" He stepped back.

"Not at all." Avrin held out a small horn. "If you see anyone, give three short blasts on this – only I will hear it."

Worten took the thing and blew. Sapphire heard nothing, but Avrin covered his ears as though in pain.

"Sorry. What if it's the flameys?"

"Same thing. And after the first three, pause for three beats, then give one blast per creature so I know how many there are."

"Why can't Bod do it?" His tone turned sulky.

"He'll be doing the same from the west and south."

Worten opened his mouth to voice more protests, but Avrin whispered in his ear. Although Sapphire couldn't make out the words, it obviously satisfied him as he scuttled off to hide in the bush.

The dwarf king led them down a path which followed the curve of the river until they reached another large bush where Bod grumbled even longer and louder. Avrin made no attempt to assuage his complaints, ordering him to take up his post and telling him to wait there for his signal.

As they headed to the heart of the wood, he explained more about the tree king. "He speaks directly into your mind, but beware, his speech is much slower than ours – unbearably so. Wait a few beats after you think he's finished, because there's no surer way of annoying him than interrupting mid-speech, or even mid-sentence."

"How will I know when he's truly finished?"

"If you're careful, you might sense the moment he withdraws from your mind. It took me a while to get used to it, but it's well worth the effort."

Even as he said it, Sapphire felt a peculiar sensation in her head, although it didn't hurt as much as a headache. She watched Avrin take the left path where it forked, but something told her this was wrong as the right-hand branch glimmered with a pale green glow. "I think you may be going the wrong way."

"How do you know? You've never been here before."

She shrugged. "Just a feeling. You're probably right."

His eyes narrowed. "I'm sure I went this way last time, but it was heavily overgrown. We'll try your way."

Each time the path became unclear, the same glow guided them and, as the small trickle in her mind expanded to fill her whole head, she recognised it as a presence. The Ancient Oak had found her!

"Yes --- my --- dear." A pause, then more words formed slowly in her brain. "I --- sense --- a --- good --- spirit."

Avrin nudged her, whispering. "He's speaking to you, isn't he?"

Her nod said, "Yes," even as her stricken expression suggested she dare not respond aloud.

"You --- are --- a --- child." Although the ensuing pause was the longest one yet, instinct told her he wasn't done and she waited.

"Of --- the --- forest."

This time, she heard an echo of the words in her ears and she recognised the clearing as the one he'd projected into her mind. On the opposite side stood the most magnificent tree she'd ever seen and she lowered her gaze, wanting more than anything to curtsey. A glance at Avrin's deep bow had her bobbing down, bending a knee and holding out imaginary skirts like ladies of old.

"Rise --- Sapphire."

As she did, the outline of a face appeared in the bark – one she recognised as the spitting image of Sean Connery's Richard the Lionheart in the 90s movie *Robin Hood, Prince of Thieves*.

A deep chuckle vibrated and the entire clearing quivered as though sharing the joke. "Your --- reverence --- of --- nature --- does --- you --- credit. --- Many --- could --- learn --- from --- you."

Hands together as though in prayer, she bobbed another curtsey, mouthing the word, "Namaste." She was about to say thank you, when he added more.

"Especially --- Avrin."

The dwarf king stiffened and she figured he'd heard it, too, but he merely bowed, copying her humble salutation.

The oak's words returned to sounding only in her head. "Come --- closer."

The few tentative steps were not enough as an invisible force propelled her close enough to touch and her arms stretched out to do exactly that. Instead of the rough bark she expected, her fingers touched a warm, smooth surface like the skin on a man's back. She sensed his amusement as he repeated the reverent greeting.

"Namaste. Very apt. The sacred in me recognises the sacred in you."

Although his speech was still much slower than she was used to, she no longer heard the interminable pauses between each word. *Did that mean she'd slowed down to his pace?* The reason didn't matter, but the result transformed her dealings with the divine entity as he gifted her with five acorns, in their perfectly knurled cups.

"Each one of these will direct you to an item you require to complete your task."

"Thank you, you're very kind." She remembered Avrin's words. "How will I know which order to find them?"

"Have faith, my child. You will be exactly where you need to be at the exact moment you need to be there. Learn this lesson well as it applies to every aspect of your life."

"Thank you for your gifts and your wisdom. One more thing. How will I know what to do with the items when I find them?"

"Only when the five are reunited will the magic become clear."

With no warning, she returned to stand next to Avrin, although with no conscious effort on her part.

"Good --- fortune --- pilgrims."

A blink later, they were back at the clearing near the foot of the Wishing Waterfall.

Avrin studied her with a hint of antipathy in his bearing. "Well?"

"Waterfall, actually." Sapphire grinned. The pedantic, bad-dad flippancy rife in the place had infected her.

His snort held little humour. "Why are we here?"

"Oh dear. I knew there was something else I forgot to ask. He gave me five acorns but I have no idea how to use them."

Worten sprang out of his hiding place. "Well?"

She peeked at Avrin and they shared a grin while the gnome tapped his foot.

"The Ancient Oak gave me a gift to help locate the five items."

"Show me."

She reached in her pocket for the acorns and dismay hit her. "What? How can that be? He gave me five, but I seem

116

to have lost all but this one." She pulled it out.

"*Seem* being the operative word. It must be the right one." Avrin knew how magic worked.

"But what do I do with it?" She closed her fingers around it. "Wait, I'm getting a vision. Or not."

"What did you see?"

"Just the waterfall."

"*Just* the waterfall? Do you not know–"

"Of course. Water in fountains and falls has special properties like rainwater, because it's mixed with air."

"All very well, but how do we know how much we need? This will only hold a few pints." Worten produced a small water skin.

Avrin peered at it. "I could do an enlargement spell."

"But how would we carry it? If only Bod were here, he could carry a couple of gallons easily."

"This is about teamwork. If all three of us fill whatever we have, it will have to do."

"It would help if we knew what the other items are." Sapphire rolled the dice, but did not score high enough to reveal any more information, so they had to settle for what they could carry.

They'd no sooner finished when Bod ambled up, responding to Avrin's call, so they were able to fill his massive water skin.

"Which way now, Sapphire?" Worten glared at her, and she put her hand in her pocket, praying for a miracle.

# Ch 10 – Hunting Treasures

Tangled Warren

Sending many prayers of gratitude to the benevolent oak, Sapphire withdrew her hand to display not one, but two acorns. Ignoring Bod's sceptical scoff, she held one in each hand. "This one indicates a stone maze and the other a lake with a small island in the centre."

Avrin knew both areas well. "The Lustrous Lake is west of here, south of the dwarf city, but the Megalith Maze is due south."

Sapphire added the details to her rough sketch, modifying it as the others added their opinions about the boundaries. "The obvious route is through the maze first." As she spoke, the first acorn glowed as though agreeing.

As before, a relatively easy path revealed itself, guiding them around the outskirts of the wood without meeting any more obstacles. When she commented on this, Worten glared at her.

"Don't you be saying nothing about cake, now, or you'll jinx the lot of us."

"Wouldn't dream of it." Sapphire winced at the memory of the defiant claims of challenges being a "piece of cake," which had incurred extra penalties in the first journey through the labyrinth.

Avrin rolled his eyes. "Absolutely not. We need to take advantage of every lucky break."

This time, they advanced quickly aided by the correct choices at each fork being highlighted. Then they met a colourful worm, who showed them the shortest path to the centre. There they encountered thirteen enormous sarsen stones, set in a circle, and Avrin used a turn checking for booby traps before they entered. At the heart of the temple, a small slab inscribed with a perfect pentagram formed a rough altar. A walnut-sized crystal sat on each of the five points of this star, but when Wortle tried to grasp the beautiful brown one with iridescent yellow stripes, it refused to budge.

A voice in her head told Sapphire to place the acorn in the centre of the pentagram, and the Ancient Oak's voice filled their heads as it told how each of them must give up something precious in order to release the crystals.

Bod brought out his favourite stone, worn smooth from tumbling from palm to palm, calming like worry beads.

Sapphire clapped her hands. "That's exactly the sort of thing." Hesitating, she twirled the ring on her finger. "This belonged to my mother's mother – it's all I have left of her." Closing her eyes, she connected to an image of her gran, who nodded her assent. Sending her a prayer of gratitude, she pulled off the precious ring and placed it in the triangle in front of the rose quartz crystal, which glowed an even deeper pink.

"Which should I choose?" Bod studied the other four.

"Which one appeals to you most?"

"The blue one. The white veins remind me of my hair."

"It's a good choice." Sapphire smiled at him. "Sodalite is good for the throat chakra and will help you speak clearly."

When he put his beloved stone in the triangle, a blue aura lit the crystal, and his eyebrows waggled in delight.

Worten tried the same three bangles he'd offered the hermit, but the tiger's eye crystal didn't change.

With an exasperated tut, Avrin took the whole bundle and threw them on the altar. "Sorry, but it knows these aren't really precious to you." He removed them and held them out. "It won't settle for anything less than the cheap plastic tat on your wrist. You've already made it clear how much you think of it."

As Worten covered it up, Sapphire rounded on Avrin. "What about you?"

He held up a smaller version of his magic crystal, but his expression said he knew it wouldn't work when he placed it next to the amethyst.

"Where did that come from?"

"I conjured it while we stood here, using the magic of the circle, but I guess it has more than enough of that."

"Why not give one of your charmed crystals? They are obviously much more valuable."

"Because then I will only have one left, and we might need it to get us out of some great danger."

"And yet you gave one to the hermit."

"I've never regretted anything so much. They take many hours to create."

She sighed. "That's the point – everything has different value to different people depending on the emotional attachment. You must both sacrifice something which will cause you grief." As she willed him to make the right choice, Avrin donated his sacrifice, causing a purple glow and Worten shuffled over, reaching up to place the bangle.

All five crystals glowed and popped free, rolling

towards their intended recipient as the oak's voice said how each one would help. The striped tiger's eye would give Worten courage, the purple amethyst would enhance Avrin's magical powers, and the rose quartz would strengthen Sapphire's heart for the final task. The blue sodalite would help Bod speak his truth in a way which would not upset people, and the orangey-red carnelian would ground Sir Foxface, reining in his more reckless antics.

As the carnelian rolled toward her, the oak said Sapphire must keep it safe for the mini-knight, and they must all keep their crystals in their pockets for now so the crystals could transfer their particular energies. The final task would be to slip all the crystals into the skin containing the waterfall water to charge it with special vibrations. But only when they'd collected the next two items.

Their journey to the lake passed without incident, but transporting all four of them to the tiny island posed a problem. The acorn revealed they must collect five special shells from the beach, and Avrin immediately transformed into an owl and returned shortly afterwards with one in his beak, swaggering about how easy it had been. When he returned for a second one, however, it snapped in two, dropping into the lake. A third attempt saw him going over with a small pouch tied around his leg, but when they opened it, the shell had crumbled to dust. He admitted the first one had stood out among the rest as though beckoning him to choose it, but the other two hadn't.

The acorn advised how each person must select a

certain shell, so they had no choice but to cross the lake.

None of them had any experience in boatbuilding, but Avrin in his owl form discovered a hoard of flotsam and jetsam on the nearby riverbank and they fashioned a small raft and paddles to get them to the island.

As with the crystals, each questor was attracted to a particular shell, and they confirmed its validity by holding the third acorn which grew warm in their hand. When it came to Bod, however, he selected two saying the second one was for Sir Foxface.

The Maize Maze had a very different feel – instead of towering stone walls, the pungent stalks barely covered their heads and only reached Bod's chest. The sound of an argument had them scurrying to take cover in a nearby thicket as a pack of goblins paused by the entrance.

"I say we bop 'em all over the head and tie 'em up." The first voice sounded doubtful, but the second was evil.

"Nah, just slit their throats."

"Can't do that; Stain wants them alive." The third voice had a hint of authority.

"But what if they fight back?"

"Get a grip, scaredy-cat. There's only three of them and some puny human girl who'll just run away crying."

"A few cuts and bruises will be worth it. Stain's offered an enormous reward for whoever brings them in."

Peering out, Avrin held up six fingers and gestured for Worten to protect Sapphire, then strode out, asking if anyone had seen his loyal goblins. Bod crept up behind, picked one up in each hand and banged their heads together. The half-ogre dispatched the next two before they had a chance to grab their weapons. Then he finally got the action he craved, as the last two charged at him, swords raised. He took them both on with the merest aid from Avrin, who tripped one of them up and kicked his sword away. When all six were securely bound and gagged, they hid them in the thicket, and Bod gave them each a good clout to knock them unconscious.

The journey through the maze saw them diverting to avoid another hunting party and, when they reached the fountain at the centre, it was every bit as fabulous as its name suggested. Their task was to collect more water, and Avrin suggested using an enlargement spell, but this would require the final charmed crystal, leaving them vulnerable. After a short discussion, they agreed, and all drank from Worten's small skin, emptying it.

Avrin's roll of thirteen wasn't quite enough, but Worten offered up an amulet he'd hidden in his boot. "I won this from an unlucky sprite. It grants a small boon."

Avrin glared at him. "Won by fair means or foul?"

"As fair as can be expected."

Ignoring Sapphire's warning about the dangers of unknown magic, Avrin kissed the amulet and attempted the spell, huffing a breath when it succeeded.

The fourth acorn's last instruction was to add the seashells to the fountain water, and they remembered to add their crystals to the waterfall water.

After exiting the maze, the fifth acorn told Sapphire their final item was certain herbs only found in the Fearsome Forest meaning they'd have to cross the

Ravaging River. The narrator said the nearest bridge was an hour's hike to the west, and the sun would be setting by the time they got there. However, if they headed east for ten minutes, the river forked off to create the stream which flowed into the lake, leaving it narrow enough to wade across.

"But we might get swept away by the strong current."

"Not there, a double bend slows it down."

"But we'll get drenched and can't risk lighting a fire to dry off." Worten's second objection was quashed as the sky turned black and they were soaked by a sudden downpour.

They all agreed to take the risk and made it across safely, reaching the forest in time to find a suitable place to spend the night and recharge their batteries, eating from their rations which didn't need cooking.

The following morning, after a hasty breakfast of bread and fruit, they roamed deeper into the forest which, apart from clumps of brambles which tore at their clothes and skin, was not the slightest bit fearsome. The hunt for rare herbs took several hours, and when they'd collected samples, they added them to the waters as directed.

"Well done, adventurers." The Ancient Oak's voice warmed a little. "To complete the spell, both sets of super-charged water must be emptied into the healing well, and all five must form a pentangle around it holding their crystal and shell while repeating the incantation."

"All five?" Worten's question came a millisecond before Bod's, "Pentangle?"

Sapphire rolled her eyes. "The same as a pentagon in

our world – a five-sided shape." She turned to the gnome. "He's including Sir Foxface in the five, which means we'll have to rescue him first." Amid the clamour of protests, she muttered, "At least, *I'll* have to."

# Ch 11 – Unexpected Journey

June 2022 – Season 4

The session went on longer than Jen estimated, so she called a halt, saying she didn't have sufficient material to go much further.

Ben was glad – they were all pretty tired after the festive weekend, and he knew this was when tempers started fraying and the whole thing got a bit fraught. Besides which, he could barely concentrate after what he'd discovered, and was desperate to get Georgie on her own so he could pick her brains about his incredible findings.

It seemed they were all feeling a tad peckish, so they filled a second plate, mostly with cheese, biscuits and pickles, and settled down for the day's round-up of events He couldn't believe how everyone had embraced the jubilee, but something about the whole affair brought out feelings of pride for their little island and its importance in the scheme of things. Even Kev agreed to watch, instead of suggesting something more escapist.

The news showed highlights of the pageant and, watching clips of the double decker buses, Kev and Isaac agreed they hadn't missed much. The reporter read out a message of thanks from the Queen which said she was "humbled and deeply touched" by the celebrations across the UK.

"Well that's it for another decade." Kev dusted off his hands as the girls shared uncertain glances.

"But not for this year. The Commonwealth Games are in Birmingham at the end of July. Watch out for more pomp and parades." Isaac went into lecture mode. "It's interesting how her last jubilee coincided with the Olympics being held in this country."

"But was it pure coincidence?" Kev quipped.

"I don't know, but mum always reminds me that Virginia Wade won Wimbledon in the Queen's Silver Jubilee year." Jen was a huge tennis fan. "Which reminds me, it should be starting in a few weeks."

"Followed by the Euros." Georgie added.

"No that was last year." Kev scoffed. "England lost on penalties to Italy."

"Don't remind me." Ben groaned, remembering the massive build up to the momentous final, and how Italy had only won after they managed to pull defeat from the lion's jaws of victory as one witty pundit put it.

Georgie bristled. "I'm talking about the Women's Euro's. They got postponed from last year."

"As if anyone's interested in *that*." Kev winked.

"Lots of people will be because England's hosting it this year." Georgie scowled at him.

"I'd watch it. I saw some of the Lionesses world cup qualifier against Macedonia. A ten-nil massacre." Ben's statement would normally have brought more scorn from Kev, but he held up his hands in defeat, backing off.

This left room for Isaac to sneer about the England men's team not winning anything since the world cup in sixty-six – probably the only football fact he'd absorbed from all the furore in the previous year.

~*~

Apart from the food, they left the clearing up till the

following day and, as they transported the mountain of dishes from the lounge, Ben volunteered to take down the bunting, asking Georgie to help. She agreed, a little surprised by his enthusiasm as it involved multiple trips to the attic, including a particularly tricky one carrying the trestle table. This left Jen, Kev and a reluctant Isaac to sort out the bombsite in the kitchen – no small task.

On the last trip, they took the clothes they'd borrowed, now washed as per Isaac's strict instructions, and Ben's ulterior motive became clear. When she started unzipping the sterile paper suit, he stopped her.

"Don't bother putting it on. I have a theory."

"But Isaac–"

"He's not around. Take it with you by all accounts. And we should brush off our clothes to give us extra time." He handed her a clothes brush, gesturing for her to use it while he tied a couple of carrier bags over his shoes. "If I've got this right, we'll be needing footwear."

"What do you mean?"

His eyes darted to the door. "I'll explain when we're inside." He took the brush and she tied a bag over each shoe, adrenaline pumping to raise equal measures of anxiety and excitement.

He then put the hood of the overall over his head, wearing the body like a cloak, and arranging hers to do the same. "Every little helps, gaining us a few extra minutes, but we can't turn up wearing them where we're going."

"And where's that?"

He grinned. "To infinity and beyond."

Frowning, she followed him, carrying the three outfits

as he entered the code and they stepped through the space-age opening. As she hung her outfit up in the 60s dress rack, he took the other two off her, draping them over the nearest wheelie chair.

"Hang on. Before you close it up, will you do me a favour and check any pockets of the women's clothes?"

"What am I looking for?"

"Anything which might give us a clue."

"A clue to what? Why are you being so secretive?"

Mouthing the word, "camera," he pointed at the wall behind, hiding the gesture with his body, as he spoke louder. "A clue to who might have owned this stuff. I found a keyring in the jeans I borrowed and I wondered if there might be other things."

"Like what?"

"I don't know – ticket stubs, loose change, empty sweet wrappers, that kind of thing." He went to the end of the rack which had a brown corduroy suit, shaking out the trouser pockets before checking the jacket.

"Or even worse, full wrappers." Georgie gingerly put her hand in the pocket of a raincoat. "Remember the chocolate bar in one of the boxes of kitchen stuff? It looked solid, but as soon as Jen touched it, the wrapper fell apart spreading chocolate dust everywhere."

"Exactly. I don't know if anyone's done it already–"

"How can they with Isaac keeping the place virtually out of bounds for so long? Even after the pandemic ended, he had it permanently locked up. And still has, normally. You can't think *he* would have thought to do it? Imagine the fuss when he found something squishy."

"Except it's more likely to be desiccated after all this time." He snorted. "Clearing and cleaning are among his least favourite activities. Not particularly good if you're a clean freak."

"Unless you can pay a cleaner."

"Or con your mates to bear the brunt. Much cheaper."

"I can't imagine sixties women carrying much in these tiny pockets, they were mostly for show."

"Of course. They'd stick everything in a handbag. I saw a couple somewhere."

Georgie found them on a coat hanger, coming up empty. "That's about it. Shall I do the fifties next?"

Ben checked the computer. "I don't think we'll have time to do them all – there's only twenty minutes before she boots us out. Just hang Jen's outfit in this one for now and we'll make a start on the seventies."

A tad concerned by his furtive manner, she hoped he would clue her in soon, because his expression said there was much more to this. More than anything, she didn't like working against the clock, the stress of it made her clumsy – one of the main reasons she'd chosen to work with nature. Time didn't matter to a tree whose world ran on decades and years rather than hours and minutes.

The cover on the seventies rail opened on the other side, facing the wall, and he tugged the zip, remarking how similar their outfits were to the clothes in that era.

She snorted. "Yours, maybe – with that fringed jacket."

He pulled it over his shirt, posing; then gestured at a red and black lumberjack shirt identical to the one she wore. "Except you wouldn't get a girl wearing it back then." Her glare had him backpedalling. "At least, not so much." Trying to cover up his gaffe, he gestured at the floor. "A couple of hippy bags – we should check them first."

They knelt down, out of sight of the camera, and he whispered in her ear. "I found this along with the keyring." He took out a wallet, displaying a number of large, old-fashioned notes, including a blue fiver.

She shook her head. "Are these from ..?"

"The seventies? Yep. Look, they still had a one pound note. There's some coins, too, with a couple of half-pence pieces." He pocketed the wallet.

"What does it mean?"

"I think Isaac's grandfather found a way to travel back into the past."

"What?" She jerked up, but he glanced in the direction of the camera, putting a finger to his lips.

Frowning, she lowered her voice. "I know we all wanted to believe that when we found the capsule, but really? Do you have any idea how crazy that makes you sound? You're confusing all those sci fi shows with reality. Grampy Eric could have just saved the banknotes – some people collect old currency."

"My first thought. But there'd only be one note of each denomination – there's over eighty pounds here. I checked; it's worth nearly six hundred quid today."

"Enough to buy a TV back then."

"More like a decent second hand car."

"Shut the front door. Really?"

"Really. And there's more. But we only have minutes before we get kicked out. I'm hoping I can prove this to you, but I need you to suspend disbelief for now."

"Of course you do. Isn't it one of the rules of time-travel movies that there must be some kind of time pressure just before they jump?" She chuckled.

"Absolutely." His grin turned serious. "But work with me here, please. If I'm wrong, you get to remind me for the rest of my life."

"You know I will."

"I'd expect nothing less. The thing is, I'm pretty sure I know how he did it, and I reckon there'll be something on the computer."

"How do you know all this?"

"I took a peek inside the notebook Isaac spirited away."

"But I thought that got wrecked in the flood."

"So he said, but apparently not."

"Was this last week by any chance?" She'd noticed a change in Ben's behaviour, but had been too caught up in the jubilee stuff to pay much attention.

His eyes narrowed. "Yep. I was pretty sure you'd clocked me …"

"But you haven't told the others."

"No. I wanted to find out about Grampy Eric and you seemed the best person to ask – you knew him too."

The computer informed them they had ten minutes before shut-down, so they should finish their task and prepare to evacuate.

Georgie glanced up. You didn't say how."

"He uses two dice."

"You mean twenty-sided ones like in D&D?"

"Nope. From the pictures, ordinary dice, numbered from

five to nine – can't remember what was on the last face."

"Wait." She sprang up and dashed over to the 60s shelves, searching through the toys and games and pulling out a box styled exactly like the Mousetrap and Operation games. Called Time Doctors, it had a board with pictures of Daleks and other Doctor Who foes and a complicated layout of planets and clock faces but no instructions. "You just reminded me. I meant to look for this on the net, 'cos I'd never heard of it before, but I forgot all about it." She handed him the dice, but he fumbled and dropped them onto the board where they both landed with the number seven face up.

"Butterfingers." She picked them up, twisting them in her hand. "I remember thinking …"

Brilliant light filled the capsule, cutting her short as they stared at each other. Then the lights went out and the thing vibrated, emitting a noise not unlike that of the Tardis.

Georgie wanted to ask if it was some kind of simulation, but failed because she no longer possessed the ability to convert thought energy into what was required to move the necessary muscles for her to speak. She flinched as a hand reached out to hold hers, then clung on as she realised it could only be Ben's, admiring the way he still had control over his body. Her head spun as though she'd had a skinful of cider, and sensations built inside, seeking release. Normally, when it got this bad, she'd either hurl or black out. Not that either occurred regularly, just when she lost track of her alcohol consumption – almost inevitable around Christmas and the New Year.

"Georgie. Wake up." Hands shaking her shoulders

gently; a voice from far away; hard floor beneath her.

"Not asleep." At least, she didn't think so.

"Open your eyes."

She'd thought they were open, but when she fought past whatever glued them shut, a faint glimmer helped her make out his silhouette. "Ben?"

"I'm here."

"We're not in the time capsule anymore, are we?"

"Possibly."

"What do you mean?"

"We're not in the space-age chamber, but I think we're actually in the attic, which might be a portal."

"What makes you say such a thing?"

"When your eyes adjust to the dim light, you'll see."

"No more riddles, my brain's too addled to cope."

"This room is exactly the same size and shape as Isaac's attic, but it's only got a fraction of the stuff in it – like the rocking horse and doll's house, but no furniture."

"I must have been out for ages while you spotted that."

"Minutes. I did a quick recce to check for danger."

"Is the door locked? That's surely the biggest one."

"Nope. It's a bit stiff and creaky so I didn't open it far."

"So you think we've travelled in time? To when?"

"I don't know for sure, but I could hazard a guess. More worryingly, I have no idea how to get back."

"One obstacle at a time, please." She tried to get up, but a sharp pain over her eye made her wince.

"What happened? Where does it hurt?"

"My head." Her hand went up to the source of pain.

"A migraine? I know you used to get them badly."

"Not quite. No nausea or flashing lights."

"Take it easy, there's no rush. I wish I'd thought to bring a bottle of water."

"Wait – you knew this was going to happen? You could've let me know."

"I didn't know for certain, I only managed ten minutes with the notebook before Isaac returned, and he must have suspected something, because he made damned sure not to leave it lying around after that."

"Why didn't you say anything at the time?"

"Because I needed more evidence. To begin with, I had no idea what I was reading. I thought it was for work – he's often talked about the idea of upgrading the animated dice-throw we use on some of the games."

"So what made you think it was time-travel?"

"At the back there were some tables showing the price of things in each decade, and lists of key events, like who was prime minister. Then I read a diary entry describing what I took to be a journey to a foreign country from the way it was written. But I suspect it was trip to the past."

"Why?"

"I didn't twig till Jen mentioned Virginia Wade winning Wimbledon in 1977. Until then, I'd thought VW referred to a car. But when I added it to the money–"

"Okay, I get it. Let's find out." She made another attempt to get up, this time rolling onto her knees and rising slowly, moving her head only a few inches at a time.

The attic had no skylight, and very little daylight made it through the gaps in the tiles because the roof had a layer of amateur insulation. She chuckled to herself – Grampy

Eric was way ahead of his time when it came to anything vaguely resembling what they now called green issues. And he was well into saving money, if not the planet.

Ben hovered as she made her way over to the piles of stuff. "Are you okay? Let me know if you need support."

"I'm fine. I recognise this box – it's full of crumbling blackout curtains left over from the war."

"I remember. They disintegrated when you so much as looked at them." He winked.

But this time they didn't, standing up to being lifted out and unfolded without so much as a tear.

"Well that confirms it. They haven't had the same amount of decay as in 2022, so it must be earlier."

"But how much? I can't find anything here to help."

"At least we know the house still belongs to Grampy Eric. My first thought was it could belong to strangers, then we'd be in trouble."

"You can't know for sure. This stuff could all have been here when he bought the house and he never bothered to get rid of it. He wasn't big on detoxing."

"Tell me more about him – It'll be good to know who we'll be facing."

She shrugged. "My memories are scant, and probably coloured by interactions with Isaac. I'm pretty sure he had similar OCD tendencies – or at least he'd be considered somewhere on the spectrum nowadays."

"In my head, I see him as a slightly deranged, mad-scientist-trope – like Doc Brown from *Back to the Future*."

She shook her head. "Nope. Nothing like. He was a real gentleman: quietly understated and usually serious, taking everything in but rarely speaking unless he had something worth saying. Then he could get quite passionate."

"Wow. And, I'm guessing, not very touchy-feely."

She smiled. "The complete opposite. He gave great big bear-hugs as though trying to compensate for his detachment. Isaac always hated them."

"I can imagine. I'm getting a picture – even after living with his nan for a while she gave nothing away. I wouldn't have put her with someone so introverted."

"They say opposites attract." Georgie felt a frisson at his smile which put her back into the Wild Wood when Avrin had declared his happy place was meeting Sapphire. But it was just their characters playing a part – it didn't mean anything in the real world.

He grinned. "It'll be interesting to meet her younger self – she was quite a looker. Hopefully she'll remember you–"

Georgie's hands flew up to her head. "Wait – that's not possible. I won't even be alive in this timeline – we'll just be a couple of strangers trespassing in their house."

"Shit, you're right. I hadn't thought of that. This could get tricky. We need a plan."

Thankfully, Georgie's knowledge of their extended clan meant she could pose as one of her many cousins from the travelling community. Her obvious family resemblance meant they'd be welcomed in and given bed and board with no questions asked. If he had any qualms about playing the part of her husband, Ben never let on and she primed him with a few details to make his performance more convincing.

The tricky bit was getting out of the attic without

alerting anyone but, after taking an age to open the door in tiny increments to minimise the squealing hinges, they soon recognised the more-than-just-silence of an empty house. Still cautious, but more than adept at sneaking around as a result of many paintball forays, they made it all the way to the hall to hear the sound of the key rattling in the lock. *All that effort for nothing.*

Georgie grabbed Ben's hand and led him through to the back door, which had a Yale lock, allowing them to get outside unobserved and close the door without leaving signs of their being in the house. *Unless someone spotted their footprints in the attic.*

"What the heck do you think you're doing?"

They turned to see a young Grampy Eric glaring, his arms folded. *How much had he seen?*

# Ch 12 – Silver Jubilee

June 1977 – Season 4

Ben felt a flush warming his cheeks as he tried to decide whether the man would have seen them exiting the house. His brain mushed as he scrabbled to remember how Georgie said he should address him. Thankfully, she stepped in to help.

"Cousin Eric. This is Ben, my–"

"I asked what you were doing, not who you were." The confidence in the steely tone reinforced the man's age as late thirties to early forties.

She gestured at the door. "Nobody answered when we knocked so we came round the back."

"Looking to break in were you? And what's wrong with him, doesn't he speak?"

Ben held his hands up in a conciliatory gesture. "Sorry, Mr Cordona. I promise we meant no harm, we've travelled a long way and were hoping–"

"To steal what you couldn't con out of us?" He took a step forward, the threat unmistakable.

Holding his ground, Ben figured if he truly were a member of the fierce tribes she'd described, he wouldn't be intimidated by someone smaller. The tough, wiry guy bore little resemblance to the pacifist Georgie described, and Ben didn't fancy having to get physical.

The back door burst open and a younger version of Isaac's nan wagged her finger at her husband. "Eric Cordona, what on God's good earth do you think you're doing to these people? Can't you see they're family?"

"I caught them trying to break in–"

"No, they were probably just trying the door. It's what anyone would do when people are out. Come in you two, you look famished. I bet you haven't eaten all day."

"Cousin Naomi, we're sorry for turning up unannounced, but we couldn't think where else to go."

Taking Georgie's arm, the feisty woman led her in. "I'm afraid I can't remember your name, but I'm guessing we haven't seen you for a while."

His gaze guarded, Eric gestured for Ben to enter first, but everything about the guy's stance said he wasn't convinced. *Could this have gone more wrong?*

Naomi bustled around the kitchen yet to be updated with "all mod cons," raiding the hotchpotch of cupboards for cake and biscuits – obviously home-made. They even warranted the best china teacups and saucers from a beautifully carved oak dresser which he recognised. It survived the 80s modernisation when yellow melamine units were built around it.

Ben watched as Georgie pulled on all her acting talents to drip feed their cover story – they'd been on a trip to the coast when their car had broken down. The mechanic said it would be an hour before he could look at it, so they'd popped round on the off-chance.

"What car is it?" Eric sounded more sceptical than curious.

Ben sent up a silent prayer he'd spotted the calendar next to the light switch displaying June 1977. "A Ford." He'd put a deal of effort into researching the popular cars of each decade and was prepared for more interrogation.

140

"A Cortina?"

"Nothing so grand. A beaten up Anglia which will be lucky to make it through the next MOT."

Eric claimed to prefer British cars, asserting nothing could be more reliable than his Morris Marina.

Ben gave thanks for his uncle's obsession with classic cars, allowing him to talk quite knowledgeably about certain aspects. Careful not to stray past 70s technology, he remembered power steering was available in top range models. It did the trick and the guy relaxed enough to pay Georgie some attention.

"So, Clementina's daughter, eh? I must say, the resemblance is strong. How is she?"

"I wouldn't know. We haven't spoken for a while." This at least was true, and the main reason she picked on her.

The next part of the subterfuge depended on a lot of potential snags falling in their favour. They were gambling on several factors to coalesce, allowing them to stay close to the portal until they could work out how to get back.

When Georgie suggested they should make their way back to the garage to retrieve the car, Eric suggested he could give them a lift.

"You're very kind, but it's a lovely day and we'll appreciate the chance to walk off all the delicious cake."

Georgie's slight shake of the head said this was not a good thing to say and Ben realised it could be taken as a criticism of the sweet, fattening food. He'd read that in the sixties and seventies, after the privations of post-war rationing, people didn't place the same value on the benefits of healthy eating or physical activity.

She stepped in to smooth it over. "We wouldn't like to put you to any trouble."

"It's no trouble. I've nothing more important to do."

Naomi cleared her throat. "Apart from promising to help me with the preparations for tomorrow. You know how much better you are at kneading the dough than I am."

He'd obviously planned to use it as an excuse to get out of this chore as he persisted. "It won't take long. I presume your car's at McDonough's garage?"

"Um – I didn't notice the name."

"Was it on the ring road or next to a pub?"

"The ring road."

"Yep, that's McDonough. I'm surprised he's open – most places have taken an extra day off for the jubilee."

The web of lies seemed in danger of getting out of control when Naomi once again saved the day, suggesting he called the guy first so it wouldn't be a wasted journey.

Mindful there were no such thing as mobile phones, Ben asked to use the land line, wincing at the rookie error.

"What do you mean, land line? This isn't a military installation. We have a normal phone, but you're welcome to use it. The yellow pages will have the number."

Georgie followed him out to the hall, looking up the number and Eric hovered in the doorway, watching intently while Ben figured out the strange dial on the handset. The first time he dialled it gave a repeated beeping tone.

"Engaged? Try again in a minute." Eric's advice was cut short as his wife nagged him to leave them to it and come and help.

Ben re-dialled, cutting the call short with a finger as he

pretended to speak to someone. After a whispered conversation with Georgie, they returned to the kitchen. "Bad news, I'm afraid. It needs a new alternator and everywhere's shut tomorrow so the earliest they can do it is Wednesday. Can you direct us to a bed and breakfast?"

"I wouldn't hear of it. You'll stay here. Do you need to go back to the car to fetch your luggage?"

"We don't have any." Ben had already figured this one out. "It was only supposed to be a day trip."

"Of course, you did say. It's not a problem; we can lend you anything you need."

"You're very kind. You must let us give you something." He reached for his wallet.

"Nonsense, you're family."

"At least let us help you with the bread. What's it for?"

"I promised to make a half-gross of bread rolls for tomorrow's street party. We'll let them prove overnight and bake them first thing tomorrow."

"A half gross? You mean six dozen?"

"Yes. Although a baker's dozen is seventy-eight. I'll probably do eighty to be on the safe side."

"How many people will be at this party?"

"I should have said parties. Ours will only be around thirty, but I've said I'll do it for the ones at the church and the social club."

"None in the actual streets, then?"

"Not this street, it's too busy, but we're happy to hold it here. The neighbours will be here shortly to decorate the place, and your help will be greatly appreciated."

"It would be our pleasure." His smile turned to concern

as he caught Georgie's guarded expression. Every contact with someone from this timeline was an opportunity for them to mess up, or worse, cause some kind of paradox.

"Oh dear, what kind of hostess am I? Before you start slaving, I'm sure the pair of you would appreciate the opportunity to freshen up after your long journey. Let me show you to your room."

Was she, like Georgie's gran, some kind of sorceress? It was the third time she'd said something which got them out of a hole. Except the one he was digging here was even bigger if the huge double bed was anything to go by.

Georgie grabbed the towel off the end of the bed and went straight to the guest bathroom a few doors down – the idea of an ensuite was not widespread back then. He explored, finding a closet big enough to house a shower and loo – probably a dressing room in the original house.

When she returned, closing the door, he led her into the closet to ensure they wouldn't be overheard as he explained how best to avoid slipping up. Mostly it involved listening rather than speaking, and keeping all answers to a minimum. "The same goes for questions. Wing it whenever you can, taking your cues from them. People ask questions about things they want to discuss, so give a brief answer and turn it around by asking the same thing of them. It usually works – unless you meet someone like you."

"How do you mean?"

"Sewn up tighter than a very tight thing with less likelihood of giving blood than a stone. Sorry, that didn't come out right, but you get the gist."

"You think I'm mean and miserly?"

He didn't spot the twinkle in her eye, protesting hotly. "I didn't – don't – mean anything of the sort. Reserved? Yes. Reluctant to offer opinions? Certainly. But not mean." He should have left it there, but it was important not to have her think he'd meant to disparage in any way. "You don't have a mean bone in your body, nor a miserly one–"

"How would you know what type of bones are in my body?" The flirtatious tone and accompanying body language combined to form a direct invitation for him to stare at her slender curves.

Unfortunately, his eyes obeyed, sweeping up from the ever-so-slightly out-thrust hips to the parted lips with barely a pause at the mounds swelling the breast-pockets on the red-and-black checkered man's shirt. *What the heck?* This was Georgie, the eternal tomboy, not some vamp attempting to lure him into naughty thoughts and even naughtier actions mere feet away from a huge bed.

Her throaty giggle cut through the buzzing of over-heated blood surging through his body. "If you could see your face." She patted her pockets. "What would I give for a mobile right now?"

"Do what?" He shook his head to banish the thoughts which may or may not have been influenced by their recent adventure in the Tangled Warren.

"Don't worry. I'm not about to jump your bones, I just thought we needed to discuss the elephant in the room before it got too large."

"Sorry. You know what you were saying about addled brains earlier …"

"You too, huh? I figured we ought to get a bit hot and

bothered, because that's what Naomi will be expecting after setting us up."

"You think so?"

"I know so. That pair have a healthy sexual relationship and will be expecting us to have the same."

"You're not suggesting …" He couldn't finish – not normally a problem for him.

"I'm saying we should do our utmost to make them believe we're just like them – it'll help Eric to accept you. I'm assuming you've got nowhere with getting him to open up about his experiments."

"That's just it – I don't think time-travel has entered his psyche at all yet. Maybe it happened later."

She clutched his arm. "You don't think it was because of this" – she gestured at them both – "because of us?"

"What? No. At least, I don't think so. Look, we'd better get down and help. I don't imagine we'll have a chance to investigate much until this jubilee's all over."

A grin. "Two in one week – how lucky are we?"

Luck wasn't exactly the word he'd use as he got roped in to carting heavy trestle tables around as they set them up to check they wouldn't collapse. The inevitable drizzle meant dismantling them to store in the garage overnight. Then it was up and down ladders hanging miles of plastic union jack bunting from one end of the garden to the other. Eric seemed particularly grateful to avoid this and Ben figured he wasn't keen on heights.

It finally did the trick and the man turned from grumpy to chummy, opening up about how he'd learnt to adopt the wary persona to counteract Naomi's naïve openness. "I know it's a huge part of her gypsy heritage, but she seems far too ready to welcome dodgy reprobates into our house because they claim family ties."

"I take it you had a bad experience with one of them."

"Some money went missing and it caused a big rift between us because she wouldn't let me say a word to them. I guess it's made me a little hostile. I do apologise."

"Don't worry, you had every right. An Englishman's house is his castle and so on." He inwardly cringed about his own deception, but couldn't afford to let anything slip.

"Dad, dad." A skinny lad who could have been Isaac's brother rushed up from behind Eric, tugging his sleeve.

"Brad. Trust you to turn up when all the work's done." The mild rebuke was lost on the excited lad.

"You said I could play footie 'cause school's shut."

"I didn't mean for you to be gone all day."

"Well I didn't know what you meant because you didn't say. And it's too late to take it back. Can I do a sleepover at Liam's? They're having an extra jubilee party tonight." He pronounced it "jubbly," making Eric wince as he glanced in Ben's direction.

"We've got guests tonight, son. This is Ben, one of your mum's cousins."

The lad flicked a cursory glance, mumbling something which could have been "pleased to meet you" before haranguing his dad about not wanting him in the way.

Eric struggled to hide his exasperation before giving into the lad's demands, and he shot off, victorious.

"Don't mind him; he's a good lad mostly."

"I remember being that age – the last thing you want is

to hang out with old fuddy duddies."

"I am *not* old and certainly not fuddy or duddy." Eric's stern face dissolved into a chuckle. "Whatever they are."

Ben cringed. "No idea, it was my gran's expression."

A clap on the back. "She sounds like a character."

"Aren't they all? Something about the privilege of old age to misbehave outrageously."

He barked a laugh. "You've got that right. Come on, I'm sure the girls will have something more for us to do."

After a truly sumptuous meal, they retired to the lounge where Eric opened a veneered cabinet to reveal a TV with a screen not much bigger than the twenty-three-inch monitors on Ben's desk at work. It was much too small for the size of the room, and it amused him that there wasn't a single remote in the house, so Eric had to leap up to change the channel or adjust the volume. The program producers made no attempt to smooth out the dynamic sound track, as they would in later years. They could barely hear the "expert" guests in the studio, but were deafened by the noise of the crowds waiting at Windsor Castle for the queen to "light the blue touch paper and retire," as Eric described it.

"I've never heard that expression before." Georgie forgot the no questions rule. "What does it mean?"

Eric frowned. "It's the standard instruction on fireworks. I thought everyone knew it."

"Every *man*, maybe." Naomi winked. "But us girls are never allowed near them. It's a man's job."

Georgie was saved the need to reply by the action on screen as the Queen lit the bonfire beacon at Windsor Castle. This triggered the lighting of a beacon chain all over the country, and the program showed clips of some of the key places, from St Michael's Mount in Cornwall all the way up to Edinburgh castle.

When it came to bed-time, Georgie went up to use the bathroom first and, by the time Ben got into bed, she was already snoring softly, giving no scope for awkwardness between them.


The Tuesday morning was mostly cloudy, but people were optimistic as the forecast said no rain until evening. They had more than enough to keep them busy as Georgie took over the baking of the rolls, allowing Naomi to focus on coordinating the dozens who'd turned up to help out. The extra trestle tables in the garage became like a swap shop with everyone bringing in their contributions, to be divided up between the five local venues – theirs being the largest by far, hosting closer to fifty as families brought along extra relatives.

Eric put the TV on mid-morning, and people filed in and out of the lounge where the BBC showed the procession of the royal family to St Paul's cathedral for a national service of thanksgiving alongside many world leaders and ex-prime ministers. Georgie and Ben declined to watch, having had their fill of flag-waving crowds, and were glad when Eric announced lunch was served.

The sheer number of relative strangers meant Ben could melt into the background, using the batting-questions-back technique unashamedly. Georgie struggled with crowds at the best of times and kept a low profile. He found her hiding in the pantry a couple of times, but she assured him she'd managed to eat something.

If Naomi noticed their reticence, she never mentioned it, happy to accept their desire to take over the clearing and mountains of washing-up. It earned them even more brownie points with Eric, who turned out to be quite the party animal, happy to play "mine host" to his neighbours.

When the last guest left and the clearing-up back had been well and truly broken, they sat in front of the news round-up with the mandatory cup of tea and slice of cake. Much as for the platinum one, the TV coverage had multiple outside broadcast units – although mere dozens instead of the hundreds from all over the world – showing street parties all over the country. Some villages had their own parades featuring motor vehicles decorated as historical events from Britain's past, a forerunner of the 2022 double-decker buses.

They showed a clip from the Queen's speech at the guildhall reception, where she spoke of pledging her life to the service of our people, calling her twenty-one-year-old self "green in judgement" during her salad days. Ben and Georgie swapped grins, having heard similar sentiments only days earlier. The reporter quoted four thousand organised parties in London alone, a million people lining the pavements in London, and five hundred million people around the commonwealth watching the events on live television.

Any other news paled into insignificance, apart from a mention of the average price of petrol rising to seventy-seven pence per gallon, which the reporter joked had nothing to do with the jubilee. Ben estimated the equivalent price per litre to be seventeen pence, compared to one pound seventy five in 2022 – almost exactly a tenth.

"Right. Break over." Eric jumped to his feet. "Can I press you into service once more?"

"Sure. What do you need?"

"These trestle tables live in the attic – they're a pain on my own, but with two of us, it'll be easy."

Ben tried not to react to Georgie's alarmed expression, but luckily their hosts didn't notice, and he followed the guy out, trying to figure ways of distracting him from looking at their footprints in the dust. As they hefted the first one up the stairs, Ben spotted one of the stairs – which had given way forty-five years in the future – felt a little spongy when he trod on it. He pointed this out, using it as an excuse to talk about the woodworm in his uncle's attic. "Curiously, they stayed in one beam at a time until the whole thing disintegrated."

As he'd hoped, Eric's gaze stayed fixed on the ceiling and, by the time they'd shuffled the heavy table around to make sure its weight was distributed over several joists, the floor was covered in new footprints. Just to make doubly sure, he retraced Georgie's path to the blackout curtains – her shoe size was distinctly smaller, although the plastic bags had obscured any definition.

"What's this?" Eric pulled at the dried packaging tape.

"Looks like it needs resealing if you don't want these blackout curtains to rot. Are they from the war?"

"Could be. Left by the previous owners. Been here thirty-odd years. I should sort it out, but it's one of them."

Ben declined to ask one of what, and was glad when

they'd stored the last table, having heard a weird thump after they'd deposited the second. When they took the third one in, he fully expected the others to have toppled over, but they were fine. The hackles on the back of his neck tingled, and he couldn't shift the sensation of being watched, glad when they finished. He managed to get through the rest of the evening with no more scary moments as Brad dominated most of the attention. When he got to bed, Georgie was waiting, fully dressed, her expression anxious.

"We need to figure out a way back. I'm convinced Eric hasn't caught the time-travel bug yet, but if we stay here any longer I'm in danger of saying something harmful."

"What do you mean?"

"You saw the way Brad treated them – he's a total git."

"Sounds harsh. He's like any other adolescent boy."

"Nowadays, yes, but he's way ahead of his time. I imagine most eleven-year-olds showed a bit more respect in the seventies. He gets away with blue murder."

"Because they let him. Eric gives in too easily."

"Because they nearly lost him. Naomi didn't say much, but he was very ill when he was little."

"Presumably Isaac had the same thing, then."

"No." She closed her eyes, her face scrunching up and Ben figured she was choosing her words carefully.

"Brad took drugs and got his junkie girlfriend pregnant. They continued to take them and this stunted Isaac's growth." Her breath hitched, but she continued in the same, flat monotone. "They basically dropped out, so this lovely couple brought him up, and when Eric went, Naomi found out they'd OD'd." She dropped her head.

He wanted to offer reassurance, but figured she'd flinch from his touch. "Poor Isaac."

Jerking up her head, she glared. "Poor, nothing. Seeing his father acting like a prick reminded me of all the times Isaac shat on everyone around him. He was a nightmare."

"And still is. Some of the time."

She sniffed. "Just when I think he's changed, he does something thoughtless or says something cruel and I'm right back there. A total chip off the old block."

Realisation hit Ben. "Did Brad steal stuff?"

"Why do you say that?" A beat. "I get it – junkie."

"I'm not talking about when he was older. Eric mentioned some money went missing and Naomi went mad when he wanted to blame her family."

"I can believe it." She sighed. "I reckon she suspects it was him, but she'd have no idea what he wants it for."

"You think he's using at eleven years old? We should tell them."

"And go against the prime directive? Never."

# Ch 13 – Nightmare World

June 1977/22 – Season 4

After all Ben's concerns about the route back, it happened quite naturally. They'd figured it had to be something to do with the combination of the dice and the time portal in the attic, but they needed to be alone in the house to try it out. But Wednesday was a normal day, with Eric dropping Brad at school on his way to work.

"You're welcome to stay until your car's fixed. Feel free to call the garage from here, they should be open by eight thirty, but I'd leave it till nine."

"Thanks, we really appreciate your hospitality."

He scoffed. "It's been our pleasure, and thank you for all your help – made our lives easier, that's for certain sure." He held out a hand. "I hope to see you before you go, but if not, know you are welcome here any time."

Ben shook his hand, gasping as he was dragged into a bear hug which ended with Eric clapping his back before releasing him, his eyes suspiciously moist.

Brad watched them through hooded eyes, heaving an exaggerated sigh as his father hugged Georgie, even tapping his foot like the spoilt brat he was.

After clearing the kitchen, Naomi repeated the hugs before leaving for her part time job at the florists in town. "Don't worry about locking up – leave by the back door, it locks itself after you. I hope to meet you both again."

Ben assured her they would, thanking her again for everything, but she tiptoed up to whisper in his ear. "Take care of Georgie, she's very special."

When she'd gone, he expected Georgie to quiz him about her words, but she'd gone upstairs and he found her in Brad's bedroom. "What are you doing?"

"I thought if we could find his stash we could get rid of it, or put it somewhere Naomi would find it."

"We could, but in the long run, it probably wouldn't change anything – he has all the classic signs of an addictive personality. Best case, he'll come to it at a later date, but he's more likely to steal even more money to replace it. And it might actually make him worse – especially if Eric found out."

She frowned and he could tell she wasn't convinced.

"How about we take a quick look and if we find something, decide what to do then?"

It didn't take long to find his stash and she scoffed. "A loose floorboard? Not exactly the brightest spark."

"Ouch. Judgy much? Don't forget we've had an extra fifty-odd years of films and books turning it into a trope."

"True." She opened the envelope to find condoms, a pack of cigarettes and fifteen pounds, but no drugs.

"Is that it? I expected more."

"From what you said, fifteen quid was worth a lot."

"Of course. Over a hundred in today's money."

"We could leave them a thank you note and slip a tenner in – that wouldn't break any rules, would it? Seems about right to pay for two nights' bed and board."

"And risk insulting them?" A sigh. "Alright, if you insist, but keep the note brief."

She went in search of pen and paper, and he insisted on reading it before handing over the money. "I trust you, but

I'd hate for this to come back and bite us in the bum."

She put it on the dressing table in their bedroom, and they had a final pee before climbing up to the attic, where she retrieved the dice, handling them very carefully.

"Drat. It's too dark. I need light to examine them."

She shrugged. "What difference would it make? It's not like you can make the dice land where you want them to."

"Not if they're unbiased. But you're always telling me about the power of thought."

"They had the numbers five to nine and a strange L-shaped symbol. What more do you need to know?"

"Maybe which numbers were opposite each other–"

"Five and nine, six and eight, seven and L. I first thought it was a seven which meant they all added to–"

"Fourteen. Interesting. On a normal dice the opposite numbers add to seven."

"How does that help us?"

He frowned. "Let me see the L."

Just enough light shone through the cracks so he could make it out and he groaned. "Of course."

"What?"

"It's the CRLF symbol from old keyboards."

"Say what?"

"Carriage-return, line-feed. Like a typewriter." He mimed the action of the carriage returning to the start.

"In other words–"

"Return. They used to call the enter key the return key. And the key is actually shaped like a fat L."

"So we need a return to get back." She placed the dice into his hand, cradling it to stop them falling.

"Shit. No pressure, then. What if I roll 6-5 or 8-9?"

"In theory we go to the year sixty-five or eighty-nine, but I have a hunch it needs to be a double."

"Explain."

"Remember master numbers? What year is it?"

"Seventy seven."

"What year did we come from?"

"Twenty two."

"And how old are you?"

"Thirty three. Okay, I'll buy it. So we need double return." He shook the dice between his hands.

"Wait." But it was too late, he'd already thrown and they tumbled down, spinning over and over.

"What?"

"I was just going to say make sure you pick them up again, or who knows what could happen."

The dice stopped on six and five. He snatched them up. Nothing happened.

After three minutes of nothing happening, he started shaking again.

"Wait." This time she clasped around his hands.

"What?"

"Maybe this time, don't throw them quite so hard. You don't want them to travel so far you can't retrieve them."

"Good idea. Maybe we should make barriers with our legs, and if one comes near you, grab it." He spread his legs and she did the same, forming a rough diamond shape.

"And maybe we should hold hands so we don't lose each other in the transfer."

"Good thinking, Batman. Any more?"

She shook her head.

After a quick shake, he rolled again, releasing them gently, and they quickly stopped on eight and nine. He grabbed both dice in one hand, and her hand in the other.

Another big, fat nothing.

She shuffled closer, gesturing for him to close his leg and sat parallel, facing him with a space between them for the dice to roll. Surrounding his hands with hers, she smiled. "We'll do it together, think only of double return."

"Double return, double return." He mouthed the words.

"Picture it in your mind. Both dice showing return."

As she let go, he held his hands close to the floor and opened them, willing it to be double return. When the first one landed with the return showing, his leg jerked, and the other one bounced off it, teetering between the return and the nine. It finally landed, return uppermost, and Georgie had the presence of mind to scoop them both up, holding out her free hand, which he took.

Nothing happened.

Their gazes met, hers showing identical dismay.

Then the dazzling white light blinded them and vibrations shook his body similar to a minor earthquake he'd experienced as a child. No Dr Who theme tune this time, but when the light blinked out, it was replaced by blackness and a buzzing in his ears.

"Georgie?" Her hand squeezed his and she made a hacking sound. "Are you okay?"

She tried to speak, but cough-choked instead.

"Shhh, don't try to talk. I'll get you some water." The complete blackness suggested he was no longer in the seventies attic, and he automatically reached for his phone before remembering he'd left it in the twenties attic, figuring it wouldn't work in the past. Then he recalled another feature Isaac had insisted on. "Alexa. Lights on."

Nothing happened.

Not good news. He needed to get to an edge of the room or, failing that, one of the pillars, because he could navigate his way from there. Stumbling around in the dark didn't appeal and he wondered what time of day it could be, because even at night, some manner of external light would get through the skylight. Then he remembered the blackout blinds Isaac had installed when he slept there during the pandemic. And how he'd spent ages training Alexa to react only to his voice. It was worth a try and he tuned in to his housemate's particular cadences.

This time, when he asked Alexa to switch the lights on, weak light pooled under the slim angle-poise lamp in the centre of the attic and he wanted to punch the air in relief. He couldn't get over the difference such a dim glow made. No longer stumbling around in the dark, he dashed over to where the kitchen should be to find nothing but the ancient sink unit left over from Eric's time. But it was enough, and he rinsed out a glass from the cupboard and filled it with murky water – tasting to check it was okay.

Georgie gulped it back gratefully, setting off another round of coughing which gradually subsided as she took smaller sips until she managed to speak. "Didn't you get horribly sick? It was much worse this time."

"A little bit, but not at all the first time. My head hurt, but it went away as soon as I ate."

"Where are we? Or should I say, when are we? It feels like we're back in 2019 before we dust-proofed this place."

"I would agree except for the Alexa-lamp. I didn't think he bought that up here till he moved in."

She frowned. "Not sure, he's had a number of them about the house for a while. Let's see what the time capsule" – she grinned – "says."

He nodded. "Aptly named, indeed. Maybe we already knew because we'd used it before."

Her hands rose to cover her ears. "Don't start with all the time-looping stuff, this addled brain can't take it."

With a dastardly chuckle, he approached the fake partition and opened the panel to reveal the vintage keypad. "At least this is still the same. It's thirteen eighty-eight, right?"

"Bottom left, bottom right, top middle twice – I remember pictures better than numbers."

He pressed the keys she directed, calling them out. "One, three, eight, eight – exactly as I said." But the unit disagreed, glowing red. "What the what? I typed it right, you saw me." He went to press the one again, but she held his hand just as Jen had done to Isaac.

"Wait. You did the passcode we remembered, but what if he's changed it?"

"Why would he do that?"

"I don't know. Maybe because two of his friends have gone missing and he doesn't want to lose anyone else?"

"This is the same Isaac we're talking about? Mr Altruistic, cares about everyone before himself?"

She slapped his arm. "Just because he's a selfish git

doesn't mean he can't be afraid."

"True. If courage was an attribute he'd be a minus five."

"That's harsh. Minus four, maybe."

He nudged her arm. "Brat. But you're right. We should go find out what's happening before using up all the passcode lives and locking everyone out."

Because Ben had convinced himself they'd returned to the point before they'd done up the attic, he didn't pay much attention to the rooms on the second floor being back to how they were before Isaac turned them into suites, and he popped his head around the door of the nearest bedroom to find familiar belongings, including his large desk with three monitors. Reaching the ground floor, Ben realised what had niggled. Sure, the room was the spitting image of the one he'd lived in before the seventies suite, but in a different position.

Just as his mind tried to make sense of it, Georgie drew his attention to a noticeboard calendar displaying June 2022. "That's not right, surely? I thought this was 2019."

"What's up Georgie-girl? Lost three years of your life? Must be the mead you were knocking back last night."

She stared at the guy who kinda looked like Kev, but a chavvy version of him. This Kev obviously didn't work out, stuffing quarter of a pepperoni pizza in his mouth.

"You're out of luck if you wanted leftovers from last night's party. Me an' Zac just finished the last."

*Zac?* Surely not. The guy was adamant about not using the diminutive of his name, berating it as vulgar.

Ben felt Georgie's gaze, turning to see her alarm as she stared at the figure in the kitchen who leapt up, towering over her, a grotesque parody of her cousin. One of the multiple piercings in his ear dripped a gold chain which linked to the ring through his nostril and more chains connected studs in his sleeveless leather jacket, which revealed a whole sleeve of tattoos on his left arm.

"You two been up there shagging? Any bloody excuse. And leaving Jen to do all the clearing up. Not cool, buddy." He slapped the behind of the woman at the sink, who giggled as she turned to receive his kiss.

"See ya, wouldn't wanna be ya." Thumping Ben's arm, he leered at Georgie and then hustled after Kev-not-Kev, hollering for him to wait up.

A Stepford-wife version of Jen wiped her hands on her pinafore, assuring them she didn't mind. "Now you're up, can I get you some breakfast? A fry-up or muffins and croissants?"

"Um, just tea and toast will be fine, but we can do it." Georgie picked up the kettle to fill.

"Oh it's no bother at all. You know how I like to take care of you all. How about a bacon butty?"

Ben's mouth watered at the idea and she spotted it. "Who doesn't love one of those? And I've got those herby sausages you like, Georgie – do you want one or two?"

Her grimace indicated how little it appealed, but she quashed it. "Toast will be fine. Maybe a croissant."

"Perfect. There's one left in the oven."

The only way Ben could get through the excruciating torment of seeing his smart, razor-witted friend reduced to a robot version of herself was with a task. But she seemed shocked by the idea of a man helping out in the kitchen so

162

he muttered about needing the loo, taking the opportunity to peek into some of the other rooms.

It had mostly returned to the state before Isaac's nan died and they'd given it a makeover. The tatty condition of the furniture suggested either the current residents were *not* on substantial salaries at Gaming UK, or they spent all their money on things other than home improvements.

Come to think of it, why was no-one working today? If it was indeed Monday 6th June, the day they'd left. He got his answer on return as Stepford-Jen greeted him.

"Here he is. I was thinking of doing a roast dinner – it *is* Sunday after all." A giggle. "But Zac didn't seem keen and Kev said he'd prefer a curry. What about you?"

"I'll eat anything – which is easier?"

"They're all easy. Which do you prefer?"

"Not sure. How about you?" He turned to Georgie, willing her to say something about a veggie option.

Jen patted her shoulder. "Georgie doesn't mind, she'll follow whatever the boys decide, won't you, love?"

Gritted teeth were involved in Georgie's response as her eyes pleaded with Ben to get her out of this nightmare. "Curry sounds great. Can I help?"

"Only if Ben wants to join the boys in the cellar. They have a pool tournament going on down there."

Ben shook his head – he could think of nothing worse.

"In that case, I've got this covered. Why don't you two lovebirds watch a slushy movie?" A wink. "Or something."

"Sounds good to me." Ben held out his hand. "Come on, love." Closing his ears to the gushing sounds bordering on clucking as robot-Jen hugged herself, he led Georgie out, stopping by the door to the cellar, from where they could hear drunken singing along to Status Quo's *Caroline*. *Good call.*

They sped up to the attic, where he shut the door behind them with a sigh of relief and sank down on the floor, requesting some light from Alexa. Closing his eyes, he went back through the time he'd spent in 1977, trying to figure anything they'd done which could have resulted in this completely skewed reality. He'd been scrupulous about not alerting Eric or Naomi to their time-travelling activities, and had hardly spoken to anyone else.

Except Brad. Could they have done something by finding the stash in his room? But he'd put it back exactly as they'd found it. *Hadn't he?* Replaying the moment, he was convinced Georgie couldn't have removed one of the notes as she'd wanted to. It surely couldn't be the tenner they'd left for their keep – unless it made Eric suspicious.

She put a hand on his arm. "It wasn't you it was me."

He glared at her. "What did you do? Please tell me you didn't mention anything to Naomi." The two of them *had* spent quite a bit of time together.

"No." The vehemence suggested she wasn't that daft. "At least, not directly." She quailed at his stern glare. "I-I wrote another note suggesting they kept an eye on Brad in the future because he had the potential to go off the rails."

"Is that it?" He waited.

She glanced away, huffing a sigh. "I mentioned how taking certain drugs could lead to problems, like Thalidomide. I hoped it might be enough."

"Enough to do what? Turn Isaac from a slightly stunted

164

pedant into a chauvinistic arsehole? Not to mention the knock-on effect with Chavvy-Kev and Stepford-Jen."

"You can't blame me for them. Changing Isaac's childhood couldn't possibly have affected Kev and Jen."

"Couldn't it? You don't know that at all. The whole chaos-theory butterfly-effect."

"Sorry, sorry, sorry. I'm feeling bad enough without you going on about it."

He hadn't even started, but saw no point upsetting her further. "You *should* feel bad."

"I do, honestly. Can we go back and fix it?"

"How? You think if we roll two sevens from here we'll go back to exactly the same point in the time-space continuum as where we were a few hours ago? We've already changed things simply by interacting with the people in this universe."

"True. But the longer we leave it the less likely we'll be able to fix it."

"We've probably already missed the viable window–"

"Can we just try, please?" She retrieved the dice, pressing them into his hand.

"Okay, but if it doesn't–"

"Don't even think like that. It *will* work and take us back to seventy-seven."

"Maybe you should hold the dice this time."

She nodded eagerly holding out her hands for them, but as before, they fell from his grasp, rolling over and over.

Even as she gasped, Georgie willed the dice to fall with two sevens and, when they did, snatched them up and reached for Ben. But he was nowhere to be seen.

# Ch 14 – Another Chance

June 1977 – Season 4

This time, Georgie felt none of the travel-sickness she'd experienced on the first two jumps, which was curious. Peering around the dimly-lit room, she recognised the surroundings as being Eric's attic, but with no central structure hiding the time capsule. A quick glance revealed many similar things they'd seen in the seventies, which was good, but exactly when? The stuff had been there a while, and it could have looked the same for decades.

She remembered the furniture – especially the wardrobe with the glorious walnut inlays, but could find no sign of it, which meant it was definitely in the previous millennium before Eric left. Returning to the first section, the box containing blackout curtain caught her eye, and a closer inspection showed the box was no longer sealed.

Voices outside had her scurrying for cover, and she peeked from behind the doll's house to see Ben and Eric carrying a trestle table, which pinned it to Tuesday the seventh. She watched as Ben played a dodgy game of misdirection while he carefully obscured the traces from their initial sortie into the attic. *Clever.* She remembered from the third Harry Potter it was important that if two versions of a person ended up in the same time-line, they must never interact. As they brought the second table, she hoped like crazy the version of Ben she'd just lost wouldn't show up until this one was well out of the way.

As ever, the tricksy universe had a lesson to teach about the power of thought and, moments after the pair exited, her Ben tumbled to the floor.

This time, the travel effects got to him as he coughed and retched, unable to support his body weight. Trying to get him under cover, she prayed the pair outside hadn't heard, even as a tiny portion of her brain expected them to burst through at any moment. Remembering how he'd calmed her body's reaction with water, she felt helpless because this version of the attic had no sink. But she did have a pack of polos in her pocket – sucking on a sweet would release saliva, and mint had all manner of calming properties. She'd no sooner popped it in his mouth than the door opened and the two men brought in the third table.

The other Ben had obviously heard something, peering around as though expecting something untoward.

Her Ben, meanwhile, had slumped into what she hoped was a nap rather than any alternative. Shooing off the word coma as it bounced around the edge of her mind seeking entry, she willed them to get a wiggle on and get out. The last couple of nights taught her he snored if he lay on his back so, at the first hint of a whistle, she lifted his head off the ground onto her leg, pressing her finger against his nostril to absorb the vibration.

Other-Ben glanced over, massaging the back of his neck, visibly pleased when Eric said they'd earnt a beer.

The part of her brain which delighted in picking up on anomalies and fun coincidences registered the absurdity of the situation, hiding with Ben from another Ben, and she gazed at him fondly, jumping when his eyes sprang open.

"Did it work?" His voice cracked.

"Yep. But we're a tad early. You and Eric have just

brought the trestle tables up."

"Right. I thought someone was watching me. It was you." He shifted, and she helped him sit up.

"So we have a chance to put it right and restore the timeline. There *is* a god and he does love us."

"Someone certainly does. We just have to hide up here until our other versions have gone tomorrow and then pop down and remove the notes. Both of them."

She wanted to argue it would be okay to leave the tenner, but his frown said no. "Lesson learnt. Leave nothing but footprints and all that."

"Not even those if you can." He winked.

"True. I saw you obliterating the ones I made earlier."

"Which reminds me, I should retrieve the plastic bag shoe protectors. We should always remove them before rolling the dice in future."

"In future? You mean you think we'll do this again?"

"Possibly. Probably. I dunno. We should talk to the others about it first. And certainly find out a lot more before anyone tries."

"Eric's notebook might explain a few things."

"If we can crack the coded bits." Ben winked. "Should be possible with all of us on it. But first things first, we need to get back to our timeline."

As though the universe decided to take pity on them after all the shenanigans, everything worked to plan, allowing them to creep down – avoiding the dodgy stair – after everyone had gone to bed. After peeing, Georgie filled an empty coke bottle with water to keep them hydrated till they left. Ben set his watch alarm to wake them in plenty of time and they curled up on a pile of carpet remnants.

In the morning, they had a brief discussion about whether to stay hidden in the attic and risk being discovered by their other selves or try to leave the attic while the other pair searched Brad's room.

Reminding how fraught they'd been about the dice rolls, Ben suggested there'd be no problem with them staying, and it would refresh their memory.

"But what if we're transported with them to the wrong place again?"

He face-palmed. "Thank God one of us is thinking straight. The portal probably extends to most of the attic, so we should nip down while they return." Thankfully, he'd clocked what time Naomi had left, so when other-Ben went into Brad's room, they were waiting by the attic door and tiptoed down to hide in one of the spare rooms.

Waiting was agony, but a slight tremor accompanied the other pair's exit and they left it another ten minutes to ensure the portal had closed properly.

Desperate for no more snags, they agreed he should hold the dice with her hands encircling his, and rehearsed how they would sit and release the dice while keeping in close contact so they couldn't be separated. This prompted her to ask the question she'd suppressed, figuring he didn't want to talk about it or he'd have mentioned something by now. "What happened to you when we jumped?"

He glanced away. "Now's not the time. We should go."

Their first task was to retrieve the notes and cash, and their luck held out as, yet again, the house remained empty.

"Thank goodness. I had visions of Brad returning from school and catching us this time round."

"You mean old us? In his room?"

She held up a hand. "Stop with the paradox stuff."

"Seriously though, when we get back – if we get back to our own time, we should take some time to work a few things out before we say anything to the others."

"Especially Isaac?"

"Definitely *not* Isaac." He glanced at her. "I know he's your cousin and everything, but–"

"But nothing. He definitely knows a lot more about this than he's letting on."

"You got that right. I'm not sure I can trust him."

"I *know* I can't trust him. He's always been … never mind, it can wait until we get back."

Having rehearsed everything, it all went a lot smoother as they both repeated, "Double return," like a mantra, picturing it in their minds.

When he let go, they clasped one hand tightly and willed the dice which cooperated, landing with very little bounce, and both ending with return uppermost. Ben pocketed the dice and reached for her free hand, smiling as they waited out the "Nothing happened" for two seconds.

Bam! Blinding light – vibrations – blackout – buzzing.

They opened their eyes together, laughing as light streamed in through the skylight into the pristine attic they'd left days before. And – delight of delights – only a few feet from the chipboard partition hiding the capsule.

Ben sobered first. "I really should grab my phone, but I can't work up the enthusiasm to move."

She shook her head. "Just sit for a second and breathe. We need to let our bodies recover slowly. What we've subjected them to in the last few days isn't trivial. And, more importantly, our minds."

"You're dead right." He shook her hands. "Shee-it. What did we just do?" A scoff. "You should've heard bloomin' Isaac taunting me." He mimicked his supercilious voice. "'You didn't really believe it was a time capsule, did you? You do *know* time-travel isn't possible, don't you?' Bare-faced liar."

"Shhh." Georgie cocked her head, listening.

The door burst open. "There you are. What's going on?" Kev peered at their still-clasped hands.

They sprang apart and Ben spoke first. "Nothing. Georgie was just showing me–"

"A yoga technique for getting rid of pent up stress."

"Pah. If I didn't know better ..." A meaningful leer.

"Trust me, you don't. Know better." Ben scowled.

"We've been looking for you for ages. I already came up here once." His eyes narrowed and he shook his head. "His majesty wondered if you fancy returning to the Tangled Warren. We have some mayhem to make."

"Sure." Ben stood, helping Georgie up and she was happy her legs only wobbled a little.

When they got down, the others were already set up, and she glanced at Ben, whose subtle shake of the head confirmed they shouldn't say anything yet. Normally, Georgie would be bursting to share, but some deep instinct told her it was important to wait. Hopefully the game would distract her.

# Ch 15 – Seventy-second Suicide

Tangled Warren

*So far, so good.* Sapphire paused, taking a steadying breath as she waited for the signal, recalling the journey to date. Each of the others had used their unique skills to smooth their path through the treacherous dwarf city. Fortune had favoured as they evaded detection for the most part, with Bod coming into his own when it came to handling any hostiles they met on the way. She thought he'd developed quite a taste for the casual violence required to disarm, weaken or otherwise neutralise any potential threats.

Worten's unexpected possession of a duplicate passkey for the armoury gave them access to a hoard of explosives which they used to target prominent sites around the city.

Simultaneous explosions in the first three buildings had the militia running to fight the ensuing fires, then Avrin had flown to the fourth target – the furthest point in the castle from the tower where Sir Foxface was held. This blast caused the castle walls to tremble – her signal to light the fuse in the armoury. This detonated seconds after she'd reached the foot of the tower in time to see the two guards rushing off, presumably to investigate.

Sliding into the room, she tried to ignore her trepidation, jumping when the door swung shut behind her. The circular room was empty, with tiny arrow slits instead of windows, and the floor consisted of tessellating hexagonal tiles, containing numbers and mathematical signs.

A voice boomed out. "Welcome to seventy second

suicide. You have just over a minute to find the right path across the honeycomb, by only stepping on the correct tiles to which the answer is four hundred and twenty-nine. Stepping on an incorrect tile leads to instant death, and if you don't reach the exit before the answer disappears, the room will fill with venomous vapour and you will die. Your time starts now." In front of the door a plinth displayed the answer in digits: 429, which began to sink.

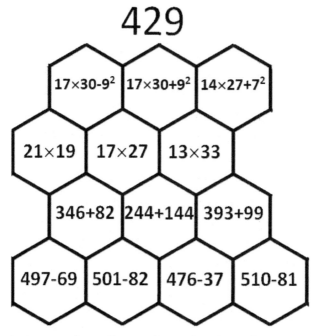

A timer on the wall started counting down from seventy, and Sapphire scanned the four tiles on the first row: 497-69, 501-82, 476-37 and 510-81. It was always quicker to add than subtract, so she added 429 to 81, getting 510, which meant the last one was correct. When she stood on it, the tile lit up and a tinkling chime said she was correct.

Fifty-two seconds remained and the next line had three additions, none of which ended in nine, so she scanned the third row which had three tiles: 21x19, 17x27 and 13x33. They were all approximately 400, and all ended in nine, so she needed to find the factors.

She remembered the strategy for finding multiples of three and added the digits: 4+2+9=15, a multiple of three, so she divided 429 by three to get 143. Jen had shown her a clever trick for finding multiples of eleven when the two outer digits summed to the middle one. So 429 was 3x11x13, which meant it had to be the last one, and the light and chime confirmed it.

The three tiles on the last row each contained a three-step calculation, the first one being $17x30-9^2$. More than half of the 429 was now obscured as the plinth sank, and only twenty-six seconds remained. A fog tried to cloud her brain, stopping her from tapping into the BIDMAS order of calculating. Shaking it off, she spotted the question was *something* minus eighty-one. A recent memory pinged and she glanced back at the illuminated tile on the first row – the *something* was 510. As soon as she figured three seventeens were fifty-one, she jumped across to the tile, which chimed, grateful when the timer stopped with thirteen seconds remaining. For once, she hadn't self-sabotaged by trying to second-guess, but instead of a fanfare, she heard only a slightly disappointed voice saying, "Congratulations."

When she stepped on the answer plinth, the door clicked open and she exited into a narrow staircase which wound around the inside of the tower until it reached the next level with an identical set-up.

As she stared at 3551, the explanation was shorter, so she only had time to recognise it wasn't in the three times table, and was forty nine less than 3600.

The first row started where the previous one left off, with four multi-stage additions, one of which jumped out straight away: 3x17+70x50. Aka 3500+51. Bingo. And only eleven seconds gone. The second row had three complex subtractions, but when she spotted the forty-nine, it was easy to work out sixty squared was 3600, so the question was $60^2$-49. As the bell chimed, a second one rang in her head because forty nine was seven squared.

The next row had three divisions, but the divisor was a single digit each time so she could eliminate them quickly simply by checking the last digit of the number being divided, none of which were correct. Although not entirely convinced, she figured if one of the top row was correct, she'd be quicker calculating them, even though they were all two-digit multiplications:

## 47x73, 53x67 and 57x63

None of them could be quickly eliminated as they all ended in one and the estimates were either 3500 or 3600. Without a pen and paper, she had no chance of checking all three in the remaining twenty two seconds. Her stomach churned and she felt nerves rushing up to freeze her brain. Then the vague bell resolved into one of Jen's mathsy mantras: the difference of two squares is the product of the sum and difference, aka $a^2-b^2 = (a+b)(a-b)$.

Instantly, she spotted the second one was 60±7 and the third was 60±3. But she'd already figured the solution was

$60^2$–49. This time she did double check: $60^2$–$7^2=(60+7)(60-7)$ =67x53. With a relieved huff, she stepped onto the correct tile with a mere three seconds on the timer. Way too close for comfort.

She climbed the stairs slowly, breathing deeply in an effort to calm her racing heart as she analysed the first two challenges. The level of difficulty had ramped up steeply, but the sprinkling of clues – like the recurrence of 3x17 and the linked questions – were there to ease her path through. However bizarre it might be.

Her pulse had just about returned to normal when she reached the third level, but her heart sank when she saw the answer: two hundred and forty had so many factors. This meant countless potential questions – she didn't stand a chance of working out all thirteen possible puzzles in time.

Again, the difficulty increased as the first row gave four sets of "product of prime factors," the correct solution being $2^4$x3x5. She made a mental note this was 16x15, hoping this might help in a subsequent question.

The next two rows involved several combinations of powers, most of which looked entirely feasible, but she got to the correct answer: $4^4$–$2^4$ by working out this was something minus sixteen, so the something must be 256 aka $16^2$ or $4^4$.

The final three were all letters: ED+2, FF–E and EF+1. Even as her brain threatened to go into meltdown, she remembered learning how computers used a sophisticated form of binary known as hexadecimal. From somewhere, she dredged up the fact F was 15, so 16x15 would be FO, and one less than this was EF, so the last one must be correct. She jumped onto the tile as the timer hit one second, but nothing happened and it kept counting down hundredths of seconds long enough for her to doubt herself.

After the longest half-second in her life, the tile lit up and the chime sounded. Everything went in slow motion as she stepped onto the plinth and, impatient with the door's lethargy, she pushed on it till the gap was wide enough for her to squeeze through.

Having survived three levels of impossibly hard questions and the increasing peril, she never expected to simply turn the key conveniently left in the lock of the fourth door to find Sir Foxface bound only with rope, tied in big, fat easy-to-untangle knots.

"Well done, my lady – as valiant as thou art beautiful. Let us escape this tower and wreak horrible vengeance."

She'd forgotten how loudly he spoke, and put a finger to his lips. "Please, my lord. You must whisper or you will draw the attention of the guards."

He reduced his volume by a tiny fraction of a decibel as he leapt onto the first step of the staircase leading upwards. "Shall we climb up to the roof? Is Avrin sending eagles to rescue us?"

She tugged him down. "Forget eagles, but if you set foot on the roof I guarantee the pterodactyls will tear you to pieces."

He shook a fist. "I'd like to see them try. I'll smite them with my mighty …" Pausing, he patted the place where his scabbard normally hung, but the belt no longer clinched his waist. "Those bounders. Stealing a man's sword."

Sapphire presented him with the dagger Avrin had given

her, and he slipped it in his boot. "A good start. What's your plan?"

"Worten discovered the servants use a secret staircase at the back of the tower, but he couldn't figure out how to get to it."

"I believe there's a hidden opening." He poked and prodded at various bits of brickwork on the walls. "Ah yes, here it is." He disappeared from view, but his voice continued. "Luckily, I have a fox's sharp hearing, and I tracked their movements when they brought food."

The opening was hidden in plain sight, only revealing itself from certain angles, but she'd seen this trick before and wasted no time exclaiming about it, following him down staircases which zigged and zagged.

At the bottom, he put out a hand to stop her, using a stage whisper as loud as a normal voice. "You must borrow my camouflage cape so you won't be seen." He took it off, holding it up with a flourish.

"But it's far too small to cover me."

"Don't worry, it won't need to."

"What about you?"

Instead of answering, he jumped into her arms, wrapping the tiny cloak around her neck where it barely covered her shoulders.

Glancing down, she could see no difference, but before she could object, he hissed in her ear.

"Hasten, my lady, time is of the essence."

Shoving away the doubts, she crept out into the courtyard, expecting the guards to have returned, but saw no sign of them. Skirting around the edge, she peered around a column to find the main gate heavily guarded. But Avrin had tipped Sapphire off about a rarely used sally port, and they managed to slip out unnoticed. She cautiously made her way into the city, expecting the alarm to be raised at any moment.

They'd agreed to meet in the house of Worten's friend, and it was only when the gnome walked straight past without a greeting she realised the cape had worked. Despite passing a number of creatures who'd not reacted to their presence, she'd still doubted it's efficacy.

Deciding to have some fun, she stuck close to Worten as he entered the house, barely making it in before the door slammed shut. But she'd had no chance to explain her plan to Sir Foxface, who sprang out of her arms, dagger raised.

Startled, Bod grappled him to the floor with much grunting, snarling and yapping as the feisty little critter fought back.

"Bod, let him go, he's a friend."

The half-ogre jumped. "Who said that?"

Avrin peered in her general direction. "Show yourself, Sapphire. How are you managing to hide?"

With a giggle, she undid the ties and removed the cape. "Sir Foxface lent me this – it's surprisingly effective."

His eyes narrowed as he inspected it. "A useful tool."

Bod had retreated to the corner of the room where he sat on the floor, taking up almost half of it. "Sorry, Sir Foxface. I swore to protect these good folk on their quest against the evil necromancer."

"Worry not, good fellow. Your actions are well met – my dagger was drawn and you had no notion whether I was

179

friend or foe." He frowned. "And your speech has changed a lot since we last tussled."

"Never mind all that. We need to get to the Enchanted Glade and work the magic. I don't suppose anyone knows a shortcut?" Worten glanced around gloomily.

"Funny you should say that." Avrin winked. "A tunnel under the city will take us part of the way, but you'll have to keep your ears closed."

"How will we see?" Worten put his hands in front of his eyes, peeking through the gaps in his fingers.

"He said ears, not eyes, dummy." Bod scoffed, and turned to the dwarf king. "Is the tunnel tall enough for me to get through?"

Avrin glanced at him. "I can walk through most of it, but you will have to stoop quite low in parts."

"Wait. Why do we have to close our ears? Explain." Sapphire fought the urge to roll her eyes at his cryptic teasing when he winked and said, "You'll see."

A short while later all became clear. The tunnel hosted a number of stone carvings – enormous, gloomy faces who spoke in droll tones, warning of dire consequences if they continued on. "Don't go *that* way. Nothing but trouble awaits anyone who takes the left path."

Sapphire tutted. "What kind of trouble?"

With a confused expression, it spoke in a normal voice. "I – I don't really know. No one's asked me before."

Hands on hips, she glared at it. Take a wild guess."

The eyebrows scuttled to form a straight line. "The – er – usual kind?"

She scoffed. "What's the usual kind of trouble?"

"I don't know. Mayhem, destruction and death?"

"You're just guessing, aren't you?"

"Because it's what you told me to do. Why are you picking on me? I'm just doing my job."

"And what exactly *is* your job?"

"To stop people from going the right way. Oops. Shouldna said that."

"Leave him alone, lady." One of the others defended him. "It's not his fault."

She rounded on him. "Oh yeah? Whose fault is it?"

"Avrin. He created all the false alarms."

Avrin stepped out of the shadows. "So you don't work for the necromancer?"

"Your majesty. I didn't see you there. What necromancer?"

"Stain. The evil sorcerer who holds the rest of my kingdom in his thrall."

"Never heard of him. But we haven't seen anyone down here in … it must be weeks."

"More like years, you old fool. No one since that Sarah girl." He peered at her. "Come to think of it, you sound alike. Is she a relative? A younger sister, or niece, maybe?"

"We're wasting time, here. We need to move on." Worten's grumble was met with a shout.

"Worten. Where have you been hiding?"

"Nowhere." He sniffed, his eyes darting around the tunnel, not quite meeting the stern gazes.

"Oh, come on. You were our best customer, leading–"

"You must be mixing me up with some other gnome."

Bod chuckled. "But we're all keen to hear about this

miscreant's misdeeds. Do tell."

"Some other time, maybe." Avrin stepped between the adversaries. For now we need to know the shortcut to the Enchanted Glade."

"That's easy. You take the right fork."

"And which one is the correct fork?"

The face looked embarrassed. "The one on the left."

"Promise me that's the truth?"

"Uh … There are three forks and you must go left, right, left, your majesty."

"Thank you. Your loyalty will be rewarded."

"So you'll send us more people to scare? I mean, warn. It gets lonely down here with no one to talk to."

"But surely you have each other?" Sapphire gestured at the other carvings.

"They're no fun. They only know a couple of phrases each and it quickly gets boring."

Bod snorted. "Not the brightest of rocks in any sense of the word."

Sapphire glared at him. "Avrin's right. You're much meaner since you learnt how to speak better. I prefer the old version; he was much kinder."

"That lumpen clod?" Bod grimaced. "He was good for nothing."

"Children, children. Stop squabbling. We need to get a move on." The king strode off, taking the left fork.

"Yes. Tally ho. Mush, mush." Sir Foxface clapped his hands and, as the sharp sound echoed throughout the tunnel, they hastened to follow.

Most of the way, they could all pass unhindered, but for

several hundred paces after the second fork, Avrin had to stoop, and Sapphire barely managed to get by. Sir Foxface had no concept of the problem, and Worten took great pleasure in gloating as he passed through easily.

Bod had to crouch so he was almost bent double, and Sapphire would have had a lot more sympathy if he hadn't grumbled and groused so much. When he actually banged his head, she tutted.

"Try putting your hand on top of your head, and don't walk so fast." She demonstrated, immediately glad as her knuckles grazed along a large, jutting-out rock, saving her head from a clout. "See? If your fingers touch the top, you need to bend down even further."

With a grunt, he followed suit and the grousing lessened.

At the third fork, Avrin chose right again, but the others reminded him what the false alarm had said.

He scowled. "I know what he said, but somehow, it feels wrong."

Sapphire considered her map. "I suppose it depends on how long we've been travelling in each direction."

"And which direction the tunnels take." Bod added. "They could run parallel to each other for all we know."

"And whether they have a way up to the surface. They could be dead ends." Worten always found a negative.

A dice roll determined Avrin's instincts were good, and the narrator confirmed it, drawing their attention to the small movement of air coming from the right fork. They followed it to a cave not far from the healing well. Before leaving the cave's cover, Avrin had Sapphire check the messages from all five acorns to ensure they hadn't missed an instruction from the Ancient Oak. This proved beneficial, reminding each questor of the part they had to play.

"But what's the spell we have to chant?" For once, Worten's pessimistic pedantry paid off – no one else had spotted the small but significant omission.

Sapphire had the bright idea of cupping all five acorns in her hands, bringing a message from the Ancient Oak, whose voice filled the cave as he chanted the words three times. "You must repeat this until the well has emptied. If anyone breaks hold, the others must throw their items into the well and close the gap.

Even as Sapphire wondered what might make any of them break hold, Bod asked that very question. Unfortunately, the king of trees had no more wisdom to share with the group. As they approached the well, however, she had a strong urge to drop all of the five acorns into it, and ran on ahead to do exactly that.

While Avrin and Bod emptied the water skins over the well as directed, she and Worten caught the precious items and distributed them to the right person. With a shell in their left hand and a crystal in their right, they linked hands around the well and chanted the phrase, "Relinquish Incantation."

After the third repetition, a screech from above heralded the arrival of the pterodactyls, but their attempts to disrupt by dive-bombing were thwarted as the five continued to recite the counter-spell. Each time the monsters tried to get closer, they stopped, squawking angrily. Sapphire had the sensation of an invisible barrier, like a force field protecting them, but the creatures kept up their relentless bombardment as though seeking to break through.

On the eleventh repetition, they head a gurgling sound and two chants later a huge belch preceded a whoosh as dazzling purple sparks erupted from the well like a massive geyser. Instead of dissipating into the ether, the stream hit the force field, now lifted high enough to encompass the entire kingdom. The magical cloud spread far and wide before floating to the ground.

Without warning, a net captured Sapphire lifting her up as the pterodactyls flapped their wings. With the link broken, the geyser stuttered to a halt, but she remembered the oak's advice and threw her charms down to Avrin. "Throw them all in," she shouted before the monstrous bird-like creatures took her too high.

A moment later, the geyser restarted and she sent a prayer of thanks to the Ancient Oak.

Any thoughts of escaping her temporary prison dwindled as she considered the effect of a fall from the equivalent height of a very tall building. Guessing the necromancer would want her alive, she examined what she knew of the evil creature or of the castle, which might aid her escape. "Very little," answered both queries. *Mostly what she'd been told.* The thought stalled her for a moment.

After being caught out a time or two, she made it a policy to give every new person who entered her life the benefit of the doubt until they gave her a reason to think otherwise. *Should she apply the same principle here?* It all came down to a matter of trust. *Now where had she heard that before?* Did she believe her fellow questors? All of them had given her reason to doubt since the quest started, but were these minor niggles strong enough to conclude they'd all been conspiring against her?

Her time for pondering ended as the castle loomed up and she was deposited on top of the round tower. Smart. *Nowhere for her to run.* She glared at the dark-cloaked figure, unable to gather her thoughts as he turned.

Avrin!

# Ch 16 – Seeing Triple

Tangled Warren

"We meet at last." The hood darkened his features, but there was no mistaking the voice.

Frowning, Sapphire peered closer and he pulled back the hood, revealing jet-black hair. Apart from that, he could have been Avrin's twin brother. Staring at the familiar – if a little twisted – smile, Sapphire had no clue how to respond. Moments earlier, she'd been holding his hand, chanting the words in an effort to reverse the enchantment created – by himself? None of it made sense.

His smile deepened, drawing her gaze to his eyes, one of which was a startling blue, the other a muddy green. But Avrin's were both deep, chocolaty brown. He could easily have flown up here in his owl form and donned a wig, but his eye colour? "Contacts." Her inner nay-sayer thwarted her yet again. She folded her arms. From her perspective, the whole thing was a puzzle wrapped in an enigma – or however the dratted quote went – and she didn't want to play anymore.

"Aren't you the slightest bit interested in the fate of your so-called friends? Surely you can't imagine a few fireworks and pixie dust will return everything to normal?" He slid a sidelong glance. "Always assuming it ever changed in the first place."

The notion was sufficiently close to her own thoughts to make her pause. Gazing steadily, she waited, knowing how much dastardly fiends liked to gloat about their cleverness.

He tutted. "Normally, teenage girls are stuffed full of

self-righteous indignation and ill-considered accusations."

Her ego-self wanted to retort hotly about not being a teenager, but that would be falling into his trap, so she focussed all her energy on showing no reaction.

"Well, I really didn't expect it to be like squeezing blood out of a stone." He continued to taunt about her gullibility, reminding her of all the times her so-called friends had let her down, while scrutinising her face.

Maintaining her indifference wasn't easy with muscles all around her mouth and eyes desperate to leak signs of exasperation, defiance and above all, indignation.

He chuckled. "Go on. The world will forgive one little eye-roll, even if your tightly-wound will-power won't."

The concentration required not to do as he suggested took more than she had and a miniscule lip-twitch escaped.

He pounced on it. "There it is! Evidence she's not made of stone, but a warm, flesh-and-blood girl. Sorry, woman."

"Claim the victory if you must, it means naught to me."

A snort. "Have you figured what it was all about yet?"

"You mean that there never was a necromancer, you merely wanted to lure me back to your nasty domain and torment me some more?"

"Ouch. Is that really what you think of him – I mean, me?"

Her eyes barely narrowed at what she surmised was an intentional slip. "A narcissistic bully with delusions of grandeur and no regard for others? Absolutely."

"I see. No redeeming features at all?"

"None I can think of."

"What about risking his life to save his people?"

Showing no reaction to his move to third-person, she scoffed. "When was this? I've seen no evidence of it."

"Not even when he flew up to recce the tower despite being badly wounded from the previous day's battle?"

Memories of Avrin's initial ghastly pallor in human form, and tattered feathers in his owl-guise surfaced and she squirmed.

"Still nothing to redeem him?"

"Courage, I guess. And some kindness – when the mood takes him."

"And where do you think the mood is taking him now?" The necromancer's nefarious grin twisted his features into their true form, which bore little resemblance to the dwarf king. His gesture had the two pterodactyls emerging above the tower's crenellations with the net suspended between them, sinking low due to Avrin's weight.

"Only you can save him by agreeing to accompany me to the underground land where darkness reigns supreme."

"Like Persephone." She shuddered.

"Oh, no. She got six months off for good behaviour. You will bear my children and warm my bed every night of the year – and there is no daylight, so that means twenty-four/seven."

"And if I don't?"

"My pets will drop him to certain death."

"Don't do it, Sapphire." Avrin's shout ended when the necromancer's out-flung arm caused a small net to fly out and fasten itself around his mouth, preventing him from speaking.

"Ignore his silly courage. You have till the count of

189

thirteen to decide. One, two, three …"

She stared at the bundle, bucking and twisting as Avrin frantically shook his head. No matter how bad he'd been formerly, he didn't deserve this fate. She stiffened. "Alright, I'll do it."

"Seven, eigh– You will? Excellent." He raised his arms to the sky. "Terry and Dax. Release him."

Instead of gently lowering him as they had her, the creatures rose, flying north in an erratic pattern which made the net tumble and spin between them. As the necromancer clapped his hands, they let go and the tightly-wound net dropped toward the barren wasteland like a missile.

Sapphire watched, transfixed, hoping to see the moment when it would unravel and Avrin's owl-form would fly out, safe and unharmed.

"Don't waste your sympathy on that wastrel – his whole life was nothing but a waste of skin."

"You cold-hearted … liar. He was worth a thousand of you – no, make it a million. You were always going to murder him, no matter what I said."

"True. But this way, you've revealed your feelings for him. You love him enough to sacrifice everything you hold dear to save his life. Now you belong to me."

"Never. I would sooner die than spend another minute with you. You're evil and ruthless and–"

"Desperate enough to plan the whole thing to see if you might ever have feelings for a beast such as me?" He removed the wig and contacts, and threw off the dark cloak to reveal the Avrin she knew and apparently loved.

# Ch 17 – Back to the Present

June 2022 – Season 4

As they stopped for a comfort break, Georgie couldn't help but spot the similarities between this campaign and her recent adventure. Both of them saw her playing roles well outside her comfort zone, in testing situations, partnering up with Ben, who appeared in two incarnations. His demeanour said he hadn't made the connection, but he did tend to get a bit method when they were in a campaign.

One thing for sure – she couldn't wait to discuss it with Jen and try to unravel these strange emotions playing havoc with her equilibrium. But not until they were truly alone with no chance of any of the lads overhearing.

Especially Ben. And Kev, who'd take the piss out of them. And Isaac, who'd find a reason to sneer.

She trotted into the kitchen to find Jen ripping open a pack of veggie sausages.

"Just the person. How many of these can you eat?"

"What with?"

"Just sausage sandwiches. I reckon we've had enough blowouts and could do with leaning up."

"What can I do?"

"Chop some mushrooms and onion rings, we'll put them in the same dish with a bit of oil and they'll keep the veggie sausages moist."

"If you cook them now they'll be done too soon."

"Automatic timer. I'll set it to start cooking in an hour and they'll be done just as we finish. If all goes to plan."

"And if it doesn't?"

"I can adjust. Simples." Her smile reminded Georgie of Stepford-Jen, and she recognised this level of domesticity and caring for others was actually a much larger part of Jen's personality than she gave her credit for. But her fierce independence, intelligence and borderline-feminist world-view kept it well hidden.

A thought struck her – they hadn't gone outside the house in the nightmare world. What if the people in that time-line were all stuck back in the mentality when chauvinism ruled and women were treated as lesser mortals? It didn't bear thinking about.

She really needed to talk it over with Ben, and she glanced at the door, wondering where he'd got to. He'd normally be down offering help by now. Maybe she could get him on his own before they resumed.

Straightening up from the oven timer, having mastered the complex sequence required to tame it into automatic subservience, Jen slid a sideways glance. "So how come you and Ben took so long up there?"

"We weren't gone *that* long, were we?"

"A good half hour longer than I'd have expected. Something you want to tell me?"

"What? Oh no, nothing like *that*." Her face reddened.

"Like what? Now I *am* intrigued."

"It's not what you're thinking. We were searching the pockets of the clothes for stuff."

"I believe you, millions wouldn't."

"We were, honestly. You can ask Ben. He found a keyring in a pocket and worried there might have been an ancient chocolate bar or something."

"Like the one which exploded into chocolate dust? Don't remind me." Another glance. "And did you?"

"Did we what?" Georgie's cheeks, which had been steadily cooling, heated up again.

"Find any exploding chocolate?" Jen chuckled, fully aware of the tease.

Isaac's noisy entrance saved her the need to reply. "Come on, ladies. The fair Georgie has just declared her undying devotion to Ben and I'm eager to know what happens next."

"I –I." The words died in her throat as Ben walked in, his blush saying he'd been suffering similar torment at the practised hands of Kev, who dragged him over, hugging the pair of them together.

"I found them on the attic floor holding hands. You're not telling me they were rehearsing for the next scene." A triumphant gloat. "Or even – what was the excuse? – doing yoga? As if, people."

As he went into a chorus of "Ben and Georgie, sitting in a tree, k-i-s-s-i-n-G," Georgie noticed the expression on Jen's face. Although her lips tried to curl into a weak smile, the disquiet in her eyes spoke of turbulent emotions.

It disappeared in an instant as she slapped Kev's arm. "What are you, twelve?"

Ben freed himself. "More like eight. Which is about when his sexual development arrested."

As the joke turned on Kev, she saw Ben's troubled glance in Jen's direction before he turned to her with an apologetic smile. "Ignore these jokers. Let's finish this."

# Ch 18 – Closure Issues

Tangled Warren

As Sapphire tried to get her head around this latest plot twist, a kerfuffle from above saw the big birds return with something in their beaks, and they swooped down, dropping Worten and Sir Foxface from heights which had them grumbling, but unhurt.

Avrin stepped aside as the pair rushed up to protect her, both glaring as he spoke. "Sorry, Sarah – I mean, Sapphire. But I had to know."

"Why?"

"Because if someone as pure and honourable as you could admit to tender feelings for me, then I'm not as worthless as people say I am."

She folded her arms. "I'm not buying it."

His uncertainty and humility were very convincing. "W-why not?"

"Because …" She paused before her nan's old platitude about leopards and spots came out. Her mum's parents were old-school types, fixed in their ways, leading to judgy, negative opinions about pretty much everything outside their – extremely narrow – comfort zone. She much preferred her gran's take about everyone having a redeeming feature. Her eyes narrowed as she recognised how he'd somehow tapped into one of her core beliefs.

"Because he's truly evil through and through?" Sir Foxface's shrug said he happily believed this.

"Or because it's all part of his shady scheme to trick you into loving him?" Worten jabbed an accusatory finger.

"You got it completely right about the bullying bit – Avrin has to pay people to laugh at his jokes."

"And as for delusions of grandeur–"

"Stop." Sapphire cut Sir Foxface off mid flow. She'd heard enough. "You're wrong. That might have been who he was the first time I met him, but I've truly seen a different side. Somewhere deep is a kind, honourable man any woman would be proud to l… to consider as a partner."

"To *love*, Sapphire? You were going to say love."

Her breath hitched as she glanced away.

Ignoring her would-be protectors as they raised fists which barely reached his waist, Avrin stepped closer, his voice seductive. "You said any woman, but what about you? Could *you* love him?"

As he whispered the last question, she raised her hand to cover her mouth.

His voice darkened. "Do you love the dwarf king?"

"I – I …" The words stuck in her throat.

"Think very carefully about what you say next. Lives depend on it."

"Whose lives? What do you mean?"

As she spoke, the door from below opened and a hoard of goblin soldiers dragged a woolly white bundle between them. Bound with heavy chains, Bod looked as though it had been a helluva fight, his tresses covered in dust, twigs and ominous dark stains. Three vicious guards shoved him closer and others surrounded all three companions, with sharp, pointy swords and spears digging into their skin.

"Answer the question. Do you love Avrin?"

Without hesitation, she straightened. "Yes I do."

"Why?"

"I love Avrin for his courage and generosity and loyalty to ingrates who barely have a good word to say about him." She aimed a glare at the trio huddling at sword-point.

"How can you possibly love a man who would do such dreadful things to you and your friends?"

"I don't believe he did. I think *you're* the Necromancer, and you've been masquerading as him for a while in your attempts to conquer his kingdom. Well it won't work."

He raised an eyebrow and she gestured at the rapidly changing lands before continuing.

"Look around you. The spell has worked and your stranglehold on the labyrinth is no more."

He waved a hand over his face, returning to the black-haired villain. "How did you know?"

Before she could answer, an object flew out of the sky, hurtling towards them. Above their heads, a flap of wings turned into the swirl of a cape as the real Avrin stood before her, clicking his fingers at the guards. Instantly, they returned to their dwarf selves and pointed their weapons at the necromancer.

The true dwarf king smiled into her eyes. "He's very good – how could you possibly tell?"

She shrugged. "I trusted my instincts. Something about him didn't smell right.

Avrin bowed over her hand, raising it to his lips. "Thank you, my lady Sapphire. It looks like your quest has ended and we've all learnt valuable lessons."

"In that case, I wish to return home."

Ignoring the protests, Avrin produced a crystal. "Your

wish is my command."

Closing the folder, Jen looked around expectantly.

"What?" Isaac pouted. "You can't leave it there."

Jen gestured. "I don't know. An open-ended final scene always leaves room for a sequel."

"But …" Isaac glared at the others. "I need closure, even if you lot don't."

"Thus spake Sheldon." Kev tapped his knuckles, accompanying the refrain known across the pond as "Shave and a haircut." *Dum-da-da-dum-dum.* Pausing, his fist a few inches above the table, he grinned, slowly sinking back into his chair, the challenge obvious.

Isaac's glare lasted five seconds before he rapped twice to complete the "two bits," sticking out his tongue. "All right, I admit I have closure issues. So sue me."

"Try pathological need for closure," mumbled Kev.

"Go ahead and write your own ending if you must, but I'm with Jen; it's over. The quest was done, the kingdom won and the bad guy vanquished. Boxes ticked." Georgie stood, stretching. "Now I need a pee and some food."

Isaac's grumbles followed her all the way to the loo as Jen sped down to the kitchen where she turned the sausages and returned them to the oven. As she stockpiled buttered toast, Georgie entered, sniffing the air.

"Mmm. Smells heavenly."

Jen offered her the plate. "What did you really think? Did I get it about right?"

"Easily. Great mix of action, adventure and mystery. Awesome twists – even Isaac didn't see it coming."

"Really?"

"Absolutely and completely. To quote Kev: Genius." She crunched down on the warm bread, her whole body savouring the sensory meltdown.

Jen joined her, helping herself to some cheese slices and red onion chutney. After washing down the mouthful with a swig of wine, she finally asked about her primary concern. "What about your character?"

"So much fun to play. I'm not cool being any kind of leading lady, and I'd be in no hurry to do it again."

"But?"

"But it kinda worked. And I enjoyed the hint of romance far more than I expected to. But I didn't appreciate those hard puzzles." She slapped her arm. "You're sick making me do stuff like that under pressure."

"Nothing you couldn't cope with, though." Jen winked.

"Huh. But never again – promise me."

"I promise." Jen's fingers were crossed behind her back.

The guys came in and Isaac cleared his throat dramatically. "So, whose turn is it next? The gauntlet is down and you have some awesome boots to fill."

Ben nudged Kev's arm. "Sounds like he's talking to you. Weren't you doing something with a castle and knights in shining armour?"

Kev mimed picking up a gauntlet. "Challenge accepted. But I warn you, it's a haunted castle, full of ghosts."

Ben grinned. "Even better. A bit early for Halloween, but you never know how long a campaign will run."

# Full map of the Tangled Warren

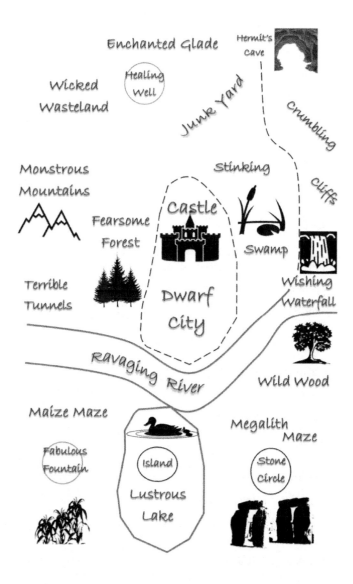

Dear Reader,

Thank you so much for reading this story – I hope you enjoyed reading it as much as I enjoyed writing it.

If you did, I'd really appreciate if you could let others know what was good/bad about it by leaving a comment on Amazon: *https://geni.us/TTtimeagain*

Thank you

Jacky Gray

To find out more about my books, subscribe to my newsletter: *https://eepurl.com/b5ZScH*

Also by Jacky Gray

**Time Doctors** – Time-Travel meets Dungeons & Dragons
*Time and Time Again*
*Just in Time*
*Time Kicks Back*

**Calamity chicks** 70s Sweethearts
*Tina's Torment* – Ugly Duckling
*Chloe's Chaos* – Goldilocks
*Linda's Lament* – Reluctant Rockstar

**Bryant Rockwell** – YA Contemporary Romance
*New Kid in Town*
*The Show Must Go On*
*Leader of the Pack*
*Edge of the Blade*
*Music was my First Love*

***Stand by Me***
***Indivisible*** – BR Boxset #1-3
***Invincible*** – BR Boxset #4-6

If you like historical-*ish* stories, Archer's magical world is now a 13-book saga featuring 3 different series:

**Nature's Tribe** – *Medieval Fantasy Saga*
***3 Handfastings and a Burial*** – Wedding-themed shorts
***12 Days of Yule*** – A Christmas-themed romance
***8 Sabbats of the Year*** – A seasonal-themed romance
***13 Esbats of the Moon*** – Dystopian origin story
***Nature's Tribe Boxset*** – Books 1-4+Bonus short story

**Hengist** – *Medieval-alternate-world Fantasy*
***Archer*** – A sensitive warrior
***Rory*** – A lonely misfit
***Reagan*** – An intrepid geek
***Slater*** – A courageous time-traveller
***Geraint*** – A reluctant heir
***Archer's Quest*** – Books 1-2+Bad Boys
***Uniting the Tribes*** – Books 3-5+Good Guys

**Colour of Light** – *the final series in the Hengist saga.*
***Context*** – Short stories of rebellion & redemption
***Chrysalis*** – Medieval magic meets modern-day mystery
***Captive*** – Modern-day mystery meets medieval magic
***Catalyst*** – Medieval magic meets modern military thriller
***Colour of Light Boxset*** – Books 1-4+Bonus short story

# Acknowledgments

Huge thanks to all the people who have supported me with constructive comments and suggestions. Special thanks to Katy, for seeing off the (many) gremlins, and Andrea and Paul for their technical expertise – really couldn't do this without you wonderful people brightening my days. Big shout out to the fabulous GetCovers designers for the awesome cover. And thanks to all those from Keith's awesome Broadhall Club who have helped out: Oso, Tracy, Georgie, Adam, Stuart, Vickie, Frank, Jonny, Andy and Duncan. A big apology to my family who have suffered the sight of me chained to my lap-top for many more hours than they ought to have endured. But the biggest thanks go to all my readers – especially those who put a review on Amazon. *Thank You.*

About the Author

Jacky Gray's first career was telecoms and after 23 years writing software, she spent 17 years teaching kids, occasionally introducing them to the joy of maths. Teaching is now ancient history – a bit like the books she writes. Well, most of them.

Jacky lives in the English Midlands with her husband and the youngest of three grown-up children. She enjoys all live entertainment, watches a lot of movies and some great TV shows like GoT, Merlin, Robin Hood, and anything remotely Marvel. She listens to a lot of Journey and Queen and reads (apologies to the adverb police) voraciously.

About the Story

This was pure joy from start to finish. What's not to like about spending time in a magical world with characters inspired by the fabulous *Labyrinth*? It was no hardship watching the movie several times, I can tell you. Any resemblance to people who think they know me is pure coincidence – I borrowed some of your story, not your life.

For a teaser of the next story, read on:

"Roll up, roll up for the scariest show in town. Be prepared to have your hackles raised, your geese bumped and your timbers shivered." The jester character leered at a frail-looking woman, who stepped back as he got right up in her face.

"I think he got the pirate script by mistake," Kev whispered in Jen's ear, drawing the trickster's attention.

"What have we here? Fancy yourself as a bit of a critic, do we, sir? Or are you just hoping your lady friend will cuddle up to you at the frightening bits?" He jumped forward so sharply his forehead almost grazed Kev's, but he was expecting it and didn't flinch back, although he had no control over his blink reflex.

"Oohhh. A hard nut, eh? Novice mistake putting a target on your back, though – unless you're one of those who craves the attention. Got you pegged, Mr …?"

"You can call me Jinx."

"Among other things. A fellow trickster, eh?" He winked at Jen. "I would keep an eye on him, fair lady. Who knows what he'll get up to in these dark, cursed passages?"

The sound of bolts being drawn back drew his attention and he leapt up onto the low wall to address the small crowd gathered at the heavy wooden door. "Ladies, Gents, and those of you somewhere in-between" – he pointed at Kev – "welcome to our famous dungeon. This journey is not for the faint-hearted, so anyone who feels they might not be up to enduring the torments within, turn back now. But don't expect a refund, you chose to pay knowing it would be the biggest fright of your life, it's clearly displayed everywhere around you." He picked on Isaac for a change. "Unless you can't read."

As Isaac prepared to give a lengthy discourse on exactly how brilliant a reader he was, the jester held up his hand.

"Don't bother to defend yourself; it's nothing to be ashamed of. Branson could barely read and look how well he did." He turned to the rest. "Seriously, guys, if you don't think you can take the pace, better to quit now. I lied about the refund – you'll get it in full. Not so once you've entered this portal – even if you bug out in the first room."

The frail woman tugged on her companion's sleeve.

He peered at her. "Any takers? This is your last chance, folks. No? Well don't say you weren't warned."

He leapt down and ran through them, scattering those in his path, to open the metal-studded door and usher them inside.

Printed in Great Britain
by Amazon